The Weaver Takes a Wife

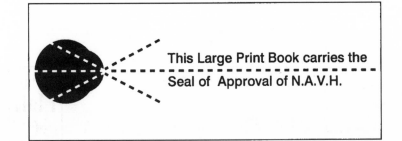

This Large Print Book carries the
Seal of Approval of N.A.V.H.

The Weaver Takes a Wife

Sheri Cobb South

G.K. Hall & Co. • Thorndike, Maine

Library of Congress Cataloging-in-Publication Data

South, Sheri Cobb.
  The weaver takes a wife / Sheri Cobb South.
      p.   cm.
   ISBN 0-7838-9304-3 (lg. print : hc : alk. paper)
   1. Lancashire (England) — Fiction. 2. Nobility — Fiction.
3. Large type books. I. Title.
PS3569.O755 W43 2000
813´.54—dc21   00-046551

To Mike, who never doubted.
You are my hero.

1

Nature's own Nobleman, friendly and frank,
Is a man with his heart in his hand.
MARTIN FARQUHAR TUPPER,
Nature's Nobleman

Of the three gentlemen occupying the box nearest the Covent Garden stage, none could honestly be said to be paying much attention to the performance, their close proximity to the proscenium arch offering a vantage point better suited for inspecting the audience than for watching the actors. Nor, in fact, could all three be called gentlemen, in the strictest sense of the word. To be sure, Lord David Markham, second son of a marquess and a rising star in the House of Commons, was deserving of that appellation; likewise Sir Aubrey Tabor, holder of a two-hundred-year-old baronetcy, was far from un-worthy of such an epithet.

The exception was their companion, Mr. Ethan Brundy, owner of a thriving Lancashire cotton mill and shrewd investor in the Funds. Alas, Mr. Brundy, though wealthier than both his compatriots combined, could not open his mouth without betraying his humble origins. But if he was aware of his failings, Mr. Brundy was blissfully undisturbed by them. He spent his money freely on such pleasures as London made available to young men of fortune but no breeding, and togged himself out in clothing that was obviously expensive, if sadly lacking in taste.

On this particular occasion, he and his friends celebrated a speech which Lord David had delivered that very afternoon to a most receptive House of Commons on the volatile subject of labor reform. The evening had begun earlier at Brooks's, where the elated M.P. had treated his comrades to supper, and had progressed thence to Covent Garden and the box in which the trio were now ensconced. Still flushed with his recent success, Lord David recounted his triumph to Sir Aubrey.

Mr. Brundy, however, as one of the primary contributors to Lord David's recent parliamentary bid, had watched his candidate from the gallery and therefore needed no second-hand account. Consequently, he soon lost interest in his friend's monologue and contented himself with surveying the crowd through his quizzing-glass, until his attention was captured by a figure in one of the boxes on the opposite side of the theater. She was tall and slender, and although she looked to be no more than twenty-one years of age, she already possessed a regal air — an impression heightened, no doubt, by the jeweled tiara crowning her honey-colored hair. She was dressed all in white, and she held her chin at a haughty angle, observing the action on stage with a bored mien. To one whose formative years had been divided between an East End workhouse and a Manchester cotton mill, she might have been Helen of Troy, the Holy Grail, and the answer to the sphinx's riddle, all rolled into one.

"Blimey!" breathed Mr. Brundy, interrupting Lord David's thrilling conclusion. "'Oo's *that?*"

Lord David's narrative faltered as both men trained their quizzing glasses in the direction of Mr. Brundy's rapt gaze. The mystery was solved when Sir Aubrey's glass lighted on the vision in white.

"Ah," said Sir Aubrey, nodding sagely. "*That,* as you so succinctly phrased it, is Lady Helen Radney. One of the *ton*'s loveliest flowers, to be sure, but the rose has thorns — in Lady Helen's case, a particularly poisonous tongue."

"They call her the Ice Princess," concurred Lord David.

"And 'appy the man 'oo melts 'er," said Mr. Brundy, his eyes never straying from the lady in question. "Gentlemen, that's the lady I'm going to marry."

Both his companions were momentarily shocked into silence. The first to recover was Sir Aubrey, who promptly fell into a coughing fit, leaving Lord David the delicate task of disillusioning his benefactor.

"Er, I would not wish to raise false hopes," he began hesitantly, raking long aristocratic fingers through light brown hair which was already growing thin, even though Lord David had yet to celebrate his thirty-third birthday.

Mr. Brundy's expressive countenance fell. "Already married, is she? I might've known."

"Er, no, as a matter of fact, Lady Helen is not married."

Mr. Brundy's brow cleared. "Well, then!"

"The thing is," explained Lord David patiently, "Lady Helen is the daughter of the Duke of Reddington. The family's pedigree goes back almost eight hundred years. They're rather a starchy lot, and Lady Helen can hold her own with the starchiest of them."

Sir Aubrey put it more bluntly. "It'll be a cold day in hell before the House of Radney allies itself with a weaver!"

"Per'aps no weaver ever asked," suggested Mr. Brundy.

"Of that, my friend, you may be certain!" Sir Aubrey said emphatically. "But to show you I'm willing to give you a sporting chance, I offer you a wager: the day you take Lady Helen Radney to wife, I'll give you a thousand pounds as a wedding gift."

"I've no need of your money," protested Mr. Brundy with an earnestness which sent Sir Aubrey into paroxysms of laughter, much to the displeasure of the party in the next box.

"Be reasonable, Ethan," beseeched Lord David. "How can you hope to marry Lady Helen Radney when you have never even met? If you will forgive me for pointing out the obvious, you can hardly expect to move in the Duke's circles."

Sir Aubrey, having by now a vested interest in his friend's courtship, was loth to give it up. "No, but you are well acquainted with the Duke, are you not, David? 'Tis simple, then. You shall perform the introductions."

Trapped between the cynical amusement of one friend and the unconcealed eagerness of the other, Lord David experienced a sudden longing for the comfort of hearth and home. Not that such comfort was likely to be found there, for although he was often seen in the company of Lady Randall, a dashing young widow and one of London's premiere hostesses, Lord David demonstrated no eagerness to surrender his bachelor status. Nor, for that matter, was he eager to set his friend's feet on a path that could lead, at best, to disappointment; at worst, it might result in heartbreak and humiliation. Mr. Brundy might be one of the richest men in England and in many ways wise beyond his eight-and-twenty years, but when it came to the workings of the *ton*, Lord David could not decide if his friend was supremely self-confident or woefully naïve. Lord David had no doubt that Lady Helen Radney could, if she chose, cut the wealthy weaver to ribbons with her razor-sharp tongue and laugh while her victim bled to death at her feet. On the other hand, a painful lesson well-learned might steer Mr. Brundy's interests toward ladies better suited for his admittedly precarious position in Society.

"Oh, very well," he agreed with obvious reluctance. "Ethan, although I will own you have a knack for getting whatever you want —"

"'Tis no special knack," objected Mr. Brundy. "All it takes is 'ard work, perseverance, and a little bit o' luck."

"To be sure, you are well qualified on all three counts, but I must admit that in this case, Aubrey has the right of it. Nevertheless, I shall introduce you to Lady Helen, if that is what you wish — although I have the strangest feeling we both may live to regret it."

As the curtain fell on the first act, many of the theater's patrons left their boxes in order to visit with those acquaintances whom they had ogled during the performance. His Grace, the Duke of Reddington, in anticipation of the crowd of gentlemen who always descended upon his box *en masse* during the intermission, betook himself to the refreshment room in search of liquid fortification, leaving his daughter to the nominal chaperonage of his son and heir, the nineteen-year-old Viscount Tisdale. Nor had the duke erred in his estimation, for he had hardly quitted the box before it filled with aspirants to the hand of the beauteous Lady Helen. Chief among these, and commonly held to be the most likely victor, was the Earl of Waverly, a raven-haired Adonis as handsome as the duke's daughter was beautiful. Unlike his competitors, who fell over one another in their attempts to reach Lady Helen before their fellows, this paragon addressed himself first to her brother.

"You here, Tisdale? I thought you still at Oxford. Is the Easter term over so soon, then?"

"No, sir, I am in Town on, er, a brief holiday," replied the viscount.

The earl cocked a knowing eyebrow. "Been sent down, have you? What did you do this time?"

Lord Tisdale grinned. "Oh, merely smuggled a pig into the provost's bedchamber — just cutting a lark, you know."

"Ah, the joys of a classical education," said the earl with a reminiscent sigh before turning the full force of his charm onto his primary object.

"Lady Helen, lovely as ever," he said, raising her gloved hand to his lips. "What think you of Mrs. Tree as Ophelia? I vow, I was almost moved to tears."

Lady Helen retrieved her hand, which the earl showed no hurry to release. "Then I must warn you against forming too great an attachment, my lord," she replied, unmoved. "She goes mad and dies in the end, you know."

"Can one be so beautiful, and yet so heartless?" the earl wondered aloud. "Tell me, Lady Helen, have you no feelings at all?"

"No feelings?" Lady Helen's green eyes opened wide. "But of course I have feelings! I have only to look at Lady Chadwick's exquisite diamond necklace, and I am filled with the most virulent envy. Could they be paste, I wonder?"

"Gems!" scoffed Lord Waverly. "Surely adorning your fair neck with jewels would be gilding the lily, my dear."

Lady Helen shrugged her white shoulders. "Perhaps I have a fancy to be gilded."

"In that case, I stand at your service," declared the earl, sweeping a bow. "You have only to say the word. What is it you want? Diamonds? Emeralds? Rubies?"

Lady Helen was startled into betraying a laugh, a silvery, musical sound that utterly banished her earlier hauteur. "As if you could give them to me, even if I so desired! All the world knows you haven't a feather to fly with."

Lord Waverly leaned closer, and his long slender fingers closed over her arm "Marry me, sweeting, and we shall have no need of feathers to fly," he murmured in a manner calculated to inform Lady Helen that he was not referring to the economic aspects of matrimony.

"If you are going to become a bore, Waverly, I shall be forced to seek more diverting company," replied Lady Helen, and promptly turned her attention to the military gentleman just entering the box. "Why, Captain Wentworth, I thought your regiment had been transferred to Tunbridge Wells! Have they tired of you so quickly?"

"Why no, Lady Helen, 'tis merely that I have already routed the enemy, and so have nothing more to do there," replied the captain.

This sally finding favor with the lady, Capta
Wentworth would have enlarged upon his imagi-
nary heroics, had the curtain not parted at that
moment to admit three new visitors. Sir Aubrey
Tabor, the first to enter the box, appeared to be
in high good humor, but Lord David Markham,
following on his heels, bore the appearance of a
man about to have a tooth drawn.

"Lord David, always a pleasure," said Lady
Helen, holding out both hands to the M.P. "Tell
me, does the delightful Lady Randall accompany
you?"

A wistful smile momentarily lightened Lord
David's melancholy expression. "Alas, no. Lady
Randall, as you must know, abhors any activity
which requires her to sit still for more than ten
minutes at a time. Lady Helen, you are, I believe,
acquainted with Sir Aubrey, but may I introduce
my very good friend and a visitor to London, Mr.
Ethan Brundy?"

"I'm sure any friend of yours, Lord David,
must also be a friend of —" Lady Helen turned
to give her hand to the newcomer, and her
mouth all but dropped open.

"Good God!" murmured Lord Waverly at her
elbow. "It's Beau Brummell's worst nightmare, in
the flesh!"

Though solidly built, Mr. Ethan Brundy was
not much above the average in height, and his
dark curly hair was too long to be fashionable.
He was not a notably handsome man, although
Lady Helen acknowledged that few men showed

to advantage beside Lord Waverly's classical good looks. Nor was Mr. Brundy precisely ugly, but any discernable beauty in his countenance owed more to a certain openness of expression than to any symmetry of feature.

More remarkable than his face or form, however, was his raiment. His evening clothes, while obviously made of the finest fabrics, were cut far fuller than the current fashion for snug-fitting garments dictated. One might almost suppose they had been made for a larger man, and yet Lady Helen had the distinct impression that Mr. Brundy's garments were not cast-offs — an impression which seemed to be confirmed by the garishly large diamond winking in the folds of his cravat. She thought of Lady Chadwick's diamonds, and wondered if his, too, were paste.

"Charmed, Mr. Brundy," drawled Lady Helen, offering her fingertips with the air of one bestowing an undeserved favor. "And what, pray, brings you to London?"

"I'm 'ere on business, I am," he replied, bowing over her gloved hand.

"Business?" echoed Lady Helen, repressing a shudder.

Mr. Brundy nodded. "I try to visit London twice a year to see to me ware'ouses. Otherwise I'm in Lancashire, where I've a m —"

"Mansion," put in Lord David, before Mr. Brundy could further demean himself in the eyes of his goddess by revealing the source of his wealth. "Two, actually, for Mr. Brundy has just purchased a London residence in Grosvenor Square."

"There goes the neighborhood," was Lord Waverly's whispered observation.

"Indeed," nodded Lady Helen, although it could not be said with certainty whether this remark was in polite response to Lord David's assertion or in agreement with Lord Waverly's.

"I'd 'ardly call me Lancashire 'ouse a mansion," protested Mr. Brundy. "Still and all, it suits me down to the ground, being close to the mill."

Lady Helen's eyebrows arched, and her smile became faintly mocking. "Then you are a tradesman, I collect?"

"Indeed I am," the weaver said proudly. "I've a cotton mill near Manchester."

"And while you are in Town, you have decided to cut a dash among the *beau monde?*"

Oblivious to irony, Mr. Brundy merely nodded. "Lord David 'as been good enough to introduce me about in Society."

"We stand forever in his debt," Lady Helen drawled. "And what do you think of the social scene, Mr. — Brundy, is it? I should love to hear your impressions."

"As to that, me lady, I find it much more to me liking now than I did just an hour ago," answered Mr. Brundy, his expression frankly admiring.

Lord Waverly drew a small enameled snuffbox from the pocket of his coat and flicked it open with his thumbnail. "Then in addition to your,

17

er, business interests, you are an aficionado of the theatre and an arbiter of taste. How vastly amusing! Pray favor me with your opinion of my signature blend, Mr. Brundy."

The weaver shook his head. "I never touch the stuff meself, but I've no objection if others do."

"Well, then, with your permission," said the earl and, placing a small pinch on the inside of his wrist, raised it to his nostrils and inhaled deeply.

Lord David had listened in silence to this exchange, all the while growing increasingly angry for the sake of his friend, who lacked the sophistication to know he was being mocked.

"I think we had best return to our box," he asserted hastily, judging it high time to intervene. "The second act is about to begin. We shall trespass on your hospitality no longer, Lady Helen."

As the curtain rose on the second act, most of the patrons made their way back to their own seats. A notable exception was the Earl of Waverly, who lingered in the duke's box long after the others had left.

"It appears you have made another conquest, my dear," he remarked to Lady Helen. "What do you think of that?"

"I think I am very glad I do not live in Grosvenor Square," she replied without hesitation. "Can you imagine having Le Brundy for a neighbor? I can readily imagine Sir Aubrey taking the man up for a lark, but I would have expected better of Lord David. Really, what can he have been thinking, bringing the creature here?"

A moment later Mrs. Tree took the stage, and Lady Helen was pleased to put Lord David and his odd acquaintance out of her mind. But twice during the second act her gaze strayed from the performance, and she was disconcerted to find Mr. Brundy watching her through his quizzing glass from across the theater. When Mrs. Tree's Ophelia finally succumbed to madness in the last act, Lady Helen hardly even noticed.

2

Vaulting ambition, which o'erleaps itself.
WILLIAM SHAKESPEARE, *Macbeth*

Alone in the sanctuary of his study, the Duke of Reddington scowled at the ledger lying on his desk. The neat rows of figures so painstakingly transcribed by his secretary were misleading, for there was nothing at all neat or orderly about the duke's current financial status. Of course, he had known for some time that he was in difficulties; Alfred, his secretary, had always taken great pains to remind him of the fact. But he had the Englishman's love of gaming, and the gambler's optimistic conviction that his luck might turn at any moment.

Alas, this conviction had proven to be groundless. After escorting his son and daughter home from Covent Garden the previous evening, he had thought to try his luck at a new and very discreet gaming establishment in Jermyn Street. The play there was deep — perhaps too deep, given his present circumstances — but the duke was not squeamish about high stakes. Unfortunately, after winning for the first half-hour, his luck had turned abruptly, and when he rose from the table just before dawn, his pockets were lighter to the tune of some twenty thousand pounds.

His investments had fared no better, and Time, which had hitherto been his ally, had at last turned adversary. Every day's post brought increasingly threatening letters from impatient tradesmen, and the threat of duns on his doorstep or an ignominious exile to the Continent was no longer beyond the realm of possibility. If Alfred's calculations were correct, it was time to begin liquidating his remaining assets. Not too quickly, of course, lest the *ton* discover his straitened circumstances and flock like vultures awaiting the kill. His unentailed property was long gone. He had staked the house in Brighton on a racehorse which had subsequently gone lame, and the hunting box in Leicestershire had been sold the previous February to fund yet another Season for his daughter.

The Duke dashed a hand over his eyes. What had he done to deserve such ungrateful children? His son, at nineteen, was still too young to marry an heiress, and while he could hardly fault the boy for his age, his daughter was quite another matter. Lady Helen, though one of London's greatest beauties, had been on the marriage market for three years, during which time she had frightened away all her most promising suitors with her damned nasty nature. With no prospect of a well-heeled son-in-law to plump up the Radney coffers, there was nothing for it but to dispose of his stables. To that end, the first of his cattle would go on the auction block at Tattersall's next week. After the horses were gone, he supposed he would begin stripping Reddington Hall, his ancestral estate, to the bare walls.

These gloomy contemplations were interrupted by a knock on the study door, and a moment later it opened to reveal Figgins, his butler, looking uncharacteristically flustered.

"Begging your pardon, your Grace, but there is a gentleman — er, that is, a *person,* sir, who desires the indulgence of a moment of your time."

The duke opened his mouth to instruct the butler to send the fellow off with a flea in his ear, but something about Figgins's manner made him reconsider.

"What is the man's name?"

"Brundy, I believe, your Grace."

"Hmmph. Can't recall that I owe the fellow money, at any rate. Send him in, Figgins."

"Yes, your Grace."

The butler sketched a hasty bow, then disappeared, to return a moment later with the visitor in tow.

"Mr. Brundy, your Grace."

Having discharged his duty, Figgins beat a hasty retreat, leaving the duke to cast a dubious eye over his caller. The man's breeches were of a bright yellow hue, and his poorly-cut blue coat of Bath superfine was worn over a garish waistcoat patterned with coquelicot stripes an inch wide. A single pearl the size of a wren's egg nested in the folds of his spotted cravat.

"Well, Mr., er —"

"Brundy, your Grace. Ethan Brundy," said this worthy, extending his hand to the duke. His Grace not being inclined to accept it, Mr. Brundy was obliged to withdraw the gesture — which he did, wiping his hand on the seat of his breeches before allowing it to drop to his side.

"And what may I do for you, Mr. Brundy?"

Mr. Brundy drew himself up to his full, albeit unimpressive, height. "I should be honored, your Grace, if you would bestow upon me the 'and of your daughter Lady 'elen in marriage." Having delivered himself of this speech, Mr. Brundy waited expectantly for the duke's reply.

The duke reached for the bell pull with the express intention of summoning Figgins to toss the impudent young mushroom out into the street, but once again he hesitated. It had been a difficult morning; surely he was entitled to amuse himself at this upstart's expense. Leaning forward, the duke propped his elbows on his desk and rested the tips of his fingers together, peering at his would-be son-in-law over his slender white hands.

"And how, pray, do you know my daughter?"

"I met 'er at Covent Garden last night, I did. We were introduced by Lord David Markham."

"I see. Well, if on the basis of one introduction, you think to align yourself with one of England's most ancient titles —"

"As to that, your Grace, I can't say as 'ow I want to marry a *title*, exactly —"

"Do not interrupt me, young man, or I shall have Figgins escort you from the premises! And what, pray, would you consider an appropriate marriage settlement, were I to agree to such a misalliance?"

"I thought per'aps fifty thousand pounds," suggested Mr. Brundy.

"Ha! Well, let me tell you, sir, that Lady Helen's dowry is less than one-tenth of that figure. *Now* are you so eager to wed her?"

Just as the duke had intended, his daughter's suitor looked distinctly ill at ease. "Er, begging your pardon, your Grace, but *I* 'ad planned on giving *you* the fifty thousand pounds."

"Look here, I don't know who you are or how you came to learn of my, er, embarrassments, but if you think to gloat over me —"

"No, no!" cried Mr. Brundy in genuine alarm. "I 'aven't 'eard anything of the sort, but if you're in need of funds, I daresay I could go a bit 'igher — seventy-five, per'aps?"

The duke was not accustomed to being mocked, and he did not take kindly to the experience. "Impudence!" he bellowed, his face turning quite purple with rage. "And where, pray, would you raise such a sum, were I to accept your suit?"

"Well, I should 'ave to consult first with me banker," confessed Mr. Brundy, glancing at the clock over the mantle. "Still and all, I expect I could 'ave the money in 'and by tomorrow afternoon."

As he listened to this speech, it gradually dawned on the duke that Mr. Brundy was quite serious. Either the man was mad as a March hare, or he was rich as Croesus. At any rate, it would be foolish to dismiss his daughter's unlikely suitor before he knew which. If this Mr. Brundy were telling the truth, he could be just the solution to the duke's financial woes. of course, there would be the devil to pay when he informed Lady Helen of the match he had arranged for her, but he was her father, by God, and if he said she was to marry Mr. Brundy, then marry him she would.

"I shall need time to consider your proposal," the duke said, rising and offering his hand to his visitor. "In the meantime, won't you join us for dinner tomorrow night? We dine at eight."

No sooner had Mr. Brundy quitted the room than the duke summoned his secretary. "Alfred, discover all you can about a Mr. Ethan Brundy — who he is, what he's worth —"

"If I may say so, your Grace, Mr. Brundy's name is well known at the Exchange. He owns a textile mill near Manchester, I believe, and his personal wealth is said to exceed half a million pounds."

"Half a million pounds, you say?" The duke's

eyes gleamed with avarice. "Send my daughter to me."

Lady Helen, having returned from Covent Garden in the wee hours, was still abed when she received the duke's summons. Knowing her father for an impatient man, she dressed quickly in a morning gown of figured muslin and threaded a blue riband through her honey-colored hair.

"Yes, Papa?" she asked, entering the duke's study a short time later. "You wished to see me?"

"Close the door, Helen, and come sit down." He waited until she was comfortably settled in a worn leather armchair before continuing. "It may come as a surprise to you, daughter, to learn that we teeter on the brink of penury."

Lady Helen's green eyes opened wide. "Again? How did it happen this time, Papa? Turf or table?"

"Do not be impertinent, miss! The how and why is not important. The fact of the matter is, it *has* happened. The question that remains is, what do we do now?"

"We could always sell the Radney jewels," Lady Helen suggested flippantly.

The duke shook his head. "They were replaced years ago with colored glass." Seeing his daughter's dismayed expression, he added irritably, "I tell you, girl, we are poised for disaster if something is not done quickly. That, my dear, is where you come in."

"Me?"

"Let us not mince words, Helen. You are

twenty-one years old. It is past time you were wed."

Lady Helen shrugged. "I have always known that I should have to marry someday. I daresay I shall have Waverly in the end."

The duke dismissed this suggestion with a snort of derision. "Waverly will never offer for you now, and you would be a fool to accept him if he did. No, my dear, I have had a better offer for you — a *much* better offer."

A prickling along the back of her neck warned Lady Helen that she would not like her father's plans for her future. "An offer, Papa? From whom?"

"Do you recall meeting a Mr. Ethan Brundy last night at Covent Garden?"

All the color slowly drained from Lady Helen's face. "Papa, no! You cannot be serious!"

"I assure you, I was never more in earnest. Alfred tells me the man is worth half a million pounds, at the least reckoning. As his wife, you would be rich beyond dreams of avarice."

An uncharacteristically wistful note crept into Lady Helen's voice as she replied, "I don't dream of avarice, Papa."

"No? Then what *do* you dream of? Your sharp tongue has frightened off most of your suitors. What, pray, are you looking for?"

Lady Helen had asked herself that question many times since her come-out, and was no closer to an answer now than she had been three years earlier. She knew that a woman of her station could not expect the luxury of a love match; her father had left her in no doubt on that head when, at the age of sixteen, she had conceived a violent *tendre* for a half-pay officer. And time had proven Papa's point: had she and her handsome captain been allowed to marry, they would no doubt have been at daggers drawn within six months. She had long since put away such fanciful notions. Still, was it too much to hope that, out of all the men who vied for her hand, she might someday find one to whom marriage would not be a punishment?

"I don't know what I want, Papa, but I am quite certain that Mr. Brundy is not it," she said emphatically.

The duke's brow lowered ominously. "I haven't the luxury to wait while you reject all your suitors for some man who may not even exist. Were it not for the protection afforded by my title, I would have found myself in debtor's prison long ere now."

"Fortuitous, indeed! What a pity the law offers no similar protection to women against other forms of imprisonment."

"What is this nonsense about imprisonment? Mr. Brundy is not, I will grant you, genteel, but he is rich enough to support you in comfort — far greater comfort, I might add, than any of your Town beaux."

"A gilded cage, perhaps, but a cage nonetheless."

"Nonsense! You want a husband who can provide for you in the manner to which you are accustomed; he desires a wife who will improve his standing in Society. The match, if not equal, would at least be mutually advantageous."

"I think you have been too long in this parvenu's company, Papa. You are beginning to talk like a tradesman."

"You mind your tongue, my girl! I'll not allow you to bankrupt us all for the sake of mere pride!"

Lady Helen arched a delicate eyebrow. "*Mere* pride, Papa? This from one who claims descent from one of the oldest families in England?"

The duke heaved a sigh, then glanced down at the ledger before him. "Unfortunately, pride won't put food on the table. Who, pray, will marry you without a dowry? Men of breeding but no wealth can't afford you, and men of breeding *and* wealth are scared to death of you. That only leaves men of wealth but no breeding, and you would be hard pressed to find a candidate with more wealth —"

" — Or less breeding!"

" — than Mr. Brundy," concluded the duke, glaring at his rebellious daughter. "This man is a godsend, Helen, and I'll not allow you to whistle a fortune down the wind."

"These are not the Middle Ages, Papa," protested Lady Helen. "You cannot force me to marry against my will!"

"Against your will, eh? Very well, then, I shall give you a choice." Turning back to his desk, the duke picked up his newspaper and flipped a few pages. "Here is a widower in Yorkshire who needs a governess for his six children. Oh, and look here! A dowager in Bath wishes to hire a companion. Duties include reading sermons aloud and walking her ladyship's pug."

"Papa —"

The duke tossed the newspaper aside and turned back to address his rebellious daughter. "You will marry Mr. Brundy, Helen, or you will earn your own living. The choice is yours."

Thus dismissed from the ducal presence, Lady Helen trudged up the plushly carpeted stairs to her bedchamber. " 'Choice,' indeed! Hobson's choice, more like," she muttered.

Had a third alternative suggested itself to her, she would have seized upon it with relish, for both of her options seemed equally repugnant. The very idea of marriage to such a man as Mr. Brundy was too dreadful to be borne, as it would make the *ton* look upon her as an object of ridicule or, perhaps worse, pity. On the other hand, if she swallowed her pride and sought employment, she would be buried alive in a position only a little higher than that of a servant, exiled forever from the glittering world of balls and routs, theater and opera, which was her birthright. How could one possibly choose between two different kinds of hell?

Throughout the afternoon, Lady Helen clung to the forlorn hope that her father's secretary would discover Mr. Brundy's reputed wealth to

be greatly exaggerated. Surely if that were the case, her father would change his mind — and if not, perhaps Mr. Brundy might be persuaded to change his. . . .

Alfred returned from his errand shortly after four o'clock, and the mercurial rise in the duke's spirits immediately thereafter led Lady Helen to suspect that her father's most cherished hopes had been realized. This suspicion was confirmed a short time later, when she was summoned yet again to the duke's *sanctum sanctorum*.

"Daughter, it is settled," announced the duke as soon as the door had closed behind her. "According to Alfred, Mr. Brundy's wealth was, if anything, understated. He dines with us tomorrow night, after which he will no doubt make you a formal offer of marriage."

Lady Helen's eyes opened wide in feigned surprise. "Alfred? Why, Papa, I didn't know he cared."

"Do not be impertinent, miss! I have written to Mr. Brundy, giving him permission to pay his addresses. You would be wise to accept them. In the meantime, I shall leave the dinner arrangements in your capable hands."

"Yes, Papa," said Lady Helen with deceptive meekness.

"Oh, and Helen —"

She had already turned to confer with the housekeeper, but her father's voice held her back. "Yes, Papa?"

"I shall hold you personally responsible to see that all goes well tomorrow night. No tricks, mind you!"

Lady Helen bowed her head. "I trust I know what is due my name, Papa."

"Good! See that you do it."

At seven o'clock on the following evening, Lady Helen paused in the doorway of the dining room before repairing to her room to dress for dinner. Surveying the scene before her, she permitted herself a smile of satisfaction. The long mahogany dining table had been buffed with beeswax until it gleamed in the light of the two large chandeliers overhead. Mrs. Overstreet, the housekeeper, had thought it odd that Lady Helen did not wish to remove at least a few leaves from the table, since only four would sit down to dinner, but the duke's daughter was adamant, and so the leaves remained. Lady Helen had further instructed that the best gold plate, adorned with the ducal crest, be used — a significant departure from the usual arrangements, which dictated that the ducal plate be used only on the most formal of occasions.

Lady Helen was most pleased with the results of her labors. Every detail, from the elaborate floral arrangement at the center of the table down to the shrimp sauce to be served with the salmon, was designed to drive home to the plebian Mr. Brundy his unworthiness to aspire to her hand. Casting a contented eye over the silver cutlery and crystal goblets, Lady Helen owned that she would not be surprised if the poor man took one look and ran all the way back to Manchester, or Liverpool, or whatever God-forsaken place he had come from.

Best of all, her father could not accuse her of subversion, for she could answer with all honesty that she had ordered the best of everything for the occasion. On this happy note, she turned and made her way to her room, blissfully unaware that in the kitchen Mrs. Overstreet confided to an enthralled Cook that Lady Helen must be that taken with the young man coming to dine, so eager was she to see that everything looked just so.

Mr. Brundy presented himself at the duke's residence precisely at eight o'clock, and was ushered upstairs to the drawing room by a dour-faced and disapproving Figgins. The duke was already there, along with a very young man whose golden coloring reminded Mr. Brundy forcibly of his intended bride, of whom there was as yet no sign.

His Grace, noting Mr. Brundy's ill-fitting evening attire, felt a momentary pang of sympathy for his daughter, but suppressed it at once. "Pleased to see you're prompt, at any rate," he said grudgingly, offering his hand to the newcomer. "Allow me to present my son Theodore, Viscount Tisdale. Theodore, Mr. Ethan Brundy. Mr. Brundy is to marry your sister."

"If she'll 'ave me," Mr. Brundy felt obliged to add.

Like most young men who had yet to reach

their twentieth year, the viscount had a fatal tendency to levity, and the thought of his haughty sister wed to this badly dressed Cit struck him as supremely funny. He offered his right hand to his prospective brother and raised his left to his mouth, hiding the grin he could not quite suppress.

If the duke was aware of the effect of his pronouncement upon his son and heir, he chose to ignore it. "Theodore will shortly be returning to Oxford, but you may rely upon both of us to do all we can to ease your entry into Society," he said. "I shall, of course, put you up for membership at White's —"

"Begging your pardon, sir, but I should find Brooks's more to me liking," put in the bridegroom.

The duke was less than pleased by this show of independence on the part of his future son-in-law. "A Whig, eh? Well, don't think your money gives you the right to dictate politics to me, or you shall soon learn your mistake!"

"Yes, sir," replied Mr. Brundy meekly.

He was spared the necessity of further reply by the appearance of Lady Helen in the doorway. She was dressed for the occasion in a high-waisted gown of palest blue satin, with pearls at her ears and throat. At the sight of her unwanted suitor, her chin rose and she looked down her patrician nose at him in much the same way one might regard a particularly repugnant species of insect.

"Mr. Brundy," she said with a nod, making the most perfunctory of curtsies to her father's guest.

He made no move to take her hand, but merely bowed and responded in kind. "Lady 'elen."

"My name is *Helen*, Mr. Brundy," she said coldly.

"Very well — 'elen," said Mr. Brundy, surprised and gratified at being given permission, and on such short acquaintance, to dispense with the use of her courtesy title.

Lady Helen would have acquainted him with his error in no uncertain terms but for the dinner gong which sounded at that moment. Biting back the retort which trembled on the tip of her tongue, she took her father's arm and led the procession to the dining room, where the foursome assumed their places at the table. His Grace, of course, was seated at the head, and Lady Helen as his hostess occupied the foot, some twenty feet away. Midway between the two sat the hapless Mr. Brundy at the duke's right, and directly across the table from him (and by far his nearest neighbor) was the viscount, although Mr. Brundy's view of this young man was blocked by a large floral arrangement. Behind each chair, a footman in full livery and powdered hair stood ready to refill glasses and remove dishes. Mr. Brundy's only visible sign of discomfiture might have been observed in the dubious glance he cast over his shoulder at this attendant, as if he suspected the man of having designs on his dinner.

The meal began with a curry soup, which was removed by a salmon in shrimp sauce, and Lady Helen noticed with no small sense of relief that Mr. Brundy neither slurped his soup nor ate with his knife. Conversation, such as it was, was desultory. Neither the duke nor his offspring were in the habit of fraternizing with tradesmen, and Mr. Brundy showed no tendency toward loquacity. Lady Helen, remembering his accent, could not feel the frequent lengthy silences to be entirely a bad thing.

The second course had hardly begun when young Tisdale, feeling it incumbent upon him to contribute something to the foundering conversation, leaned to his left and addressed Mr. Brundy around the formidable barrier of the centerpiece.

"If you will forgive my saying so, Mr. Brundy," began the viscount, "you seem rather young to have amassed a — that is, to have acquired a textile mill."

"I am turned twenty-eight," confessed Mr. Brundy, "and as to 'ow I came by the mill, well, that's a story in itself."

"Pray, indulge us," beseeched the duke, ignoring his daughter's pained expression.

"Me mum died when I was six, and I was sent to the work'ouse —" began Mr. Brundy, only to be interrupted.

"Why the workhouse?" asked Theodore. "Could not your father have taken care of you?"

"I'd no father, nor any other family."

"So you are an orphan," observed the duke, relieved to learn that there were no more Brundys waiting in the wings to avail themselves of the Radney connection.

But if the duke was pleased at the turn the conversation had taken. Mr. Brundy looked distinctly ill at ease. "Not 'ardly, your Grace."

"I don't understand."

"Well, there were men living as *might* 'ave been me dad, but me mum wasn't quite sure which —"

Here he was obliged to delay his narrative, for the young viscount succumbed to a coughing fit while Lady Helen, blushing scarlet, applied herself with vigor to the consumption of a peach syllabub.

"At any rate," continued Mr. Brundy, "I left the work'ouse when I was nine. A mill owner in Manchester — Brundy, 's name was — came to London on business, and took me back with 'im."

The duke nodded. "I detected the East End in your speech. But why London? Are there no workhouses in Manchester?"

"Aye, that there are, but Mr. Brundy'd 'eard 'e could get a better price in Town."

"Are you saying he *bought* you from the workhouse?" demanded the viscount, appalled.

"Not at all. They paid 'im to take me," he explained in a voice devoid of self-pity. Finding shocked disbelief written large upon the faces of his audience, he felt compelled to explain, "'e was paid for removing me from the parish. Fewer mouths to feed, you know."

"As a matter of fact, I did *not* know, having never had the need nor the inclination to inquire into such matters," barked the duke, uncomfortably aware of having fallen asleep during the recent Poor Law debates in the House of Lords. "You wander from the point, sir. Pray continue."

"As you wish. One day Mr. Brundy caught me changing the bobbin while the loom was still in motion. Sort of a game it was with me, to 'elp pass the time, seeing if I could beat the machine —" Seeing the baffled looks on the faces of his audience, Mr. Brundy broke off. He might as well have been speaking Russian, for all they understood. "Anyway, it was a fool thing to do. I might've lost me fingers, or worse. But Mr. Brundy took a shine to me, thinking 'ow dedicated I was, not wanting to waste time shutting the loom down. Took me off the loom that very day, 'e did, and set about teaching me the business, 'im 'aving no lad of 'is own to in-'erit. When I finished with me apprenticeship — I was twenty-one by then — 'e made me 'is partner, and when 'e died two years later, 'e left the mill to me, provided I took the name of Brundy — which I did, me 'aving no name of me own, so to speak."

Silence greeted the conclusion of this narra-tive, until Lady Helen broke it by rising from her chair. "That was quite a story, Mr. Brundy. Papa, Teddy, I leave you to digest it over your port," she said, and left the room in a swirl of pale blue satin.

"That was, indeed, quite a story, young man," said the duke after his daughter's departure. "In spite of your inauspicious beginnings, it would appear that you've done quite well for yourself. But I think we will not linger over port. If you wish to converse with Lady Helen in the drawing room, Theodore and I will join you there directly."

Mr. Brundy, correctly interpreting this dismissal as an invitation to make his proposal, bowed his appreciation and betook himself from the room.

Lady Helen, meanwhile, had been pacing the Aubusson carpet in agitation ever since she had withdrawn from the dining room. Why, her father expected her to marry an illegitimate workhouse brat! In the usual course of events, he would never have darkened her path, much less aspired to her hand. Surely after hearing Mr. Brundy's history from his own lips, her father could see how impossible a match between herself and such a man would be! Upon hearing the door open, she spun toward the sound.

"Well, Papa, *now* do you — ?"

It was not her father, however, but Mr. Brundy who stood on the threshold.

"Oh! I beg your pardon," she said stiffly, although her cool demeanor was belied by the heightened color staining her cheeks. "I thought you were my father."

Mr. Brundy, not being given to flowery speeches, cut directly to the chase. "No, I'm not your father, but I 'ope to become your 'usband. 'elen, will you do me the honor of bestowing upon me your 'and in marriage?"

Lady Helen gasped. Oh, the unfairness of it all! This abominable man had not even given her the chance to hint him away, or change the subject, or any of a dozen other methods to which she had successfully sought recourse in the past. Alas, the offer had been made, and now that it was on the table, she had no choice but to address it. Falling back upon her last line of defense, she took a deep breath and launched into a recital calculated to frighten the unfortunate Mr. Brundy out of his wits.

"Mr. Brundy, you are no doubt as well acquainted with my circumstances as I am with yours, so let us not beat about the bush. I have a fondness for the finer things in life, and I suppose I always will. As a result, I am frightfully expensive to maintain. I have already bankrupted my father, and have no doubt I should do the same to you, should you be so foolhardy as to persist in the desire for such a union. Furthermore, I have a shrewish disposition and a sharp tongue. My father, having despaired of seeing me wed to a gentleman of my own class, has ordered me to either accept your suit or seek employment. Therefore, if I married you, it would be only for your wealth, and only because I find the prospect of marriage to you preferable — but only slightly!

— to the life of a governess or a paid companion. If, knowing this, you still wish to marry me, why sir, you have only to name the day."

Having delivered herself of this speech, Lady Helen waited expectantly for Mr. Brundy's stammering retraction. Her suitor pondered her words for a long moment, then made his response.

" 'ow about Thursday?"

3

Married in haste, we may repent at leisure.
WILLIAM CONGREVE, *The Old Bachelor*

The wedding was a small affair, the guest list being restricted to family and intimate friends. The bride, though interestingly pale, was breathtaking in white satin, her honey-blond tresses crowned with a simple wreath of white roses in the style popularized by the Princess Royal. She was given in marriage by her father, while her brother the viscount looked on.

The bridegroom wore a coat of dark blue velvet over white pantaloons, and although the fabrics were of the first quality, the cut of the garments could not be said to do them justice. The fall of his cravat, while adequate, was not so elaborate as was fashionable, although some might have argued that the enormous diamond pinned into its folds more than compensated for its shortcomings. Having no family of his own, he was attended by Lord David Markham and Sir Aubrey Tabor. Also present was Lord David's particular friend, Lady Randall.

"Dearly beloved friends," intoned the bishop, "we are gathered together here in the sight of God, and in the face of His congregation, to join together this man and this woman in holy matrimony, which is an honorable estate, instituted of God in paradise in the time of man's innocency . . ."

This is not really happening to me, thought Lady Helen as the bishop read the familiar lines from the Book of Common Prayer. At any moment, I'm going to wake up and find that it is nothing but a bad dream.

But Mr. Brundy's gloved hand clasping hers was all too real, as were the vows he spoke in his unmistakable accent. "I, Ethan Brundy, take thee, 'elen Elizabeth Charlotte Katherine Radney to me wedded wife, to 'ave and to 'old from this day forward . . ."

"Helen Elizabeth Charlotte Katherine Radney, wilt thou have this man to thy wedded husband . . . and forsaking all others, keep thee only unto him, so long as you both shall live?"

Lady Helen cast a covert glance at the common, ill-dressed man at her side. No, no, a thousand times no! But even as she opened her mouth to say the words, she darted a glance at her father. His thin lips pressed together in a hard line, and his eyebrows lowered ominously. A picture of herself, clad in shapeless black bombazine and walking an obnoxious pug down Pulteney Street, swam before her eyes.

"I — I will," she said.

". . . If any man can show just cause why these two may not lawfully be joined together, let him now speak, or else hereafter forever hold his peace."

Papa will intervene, Lady Helen thought with a confidence born of desperation. He had only wanted to teach her a lesson in filial obedience; he never really expected her to make such a dreadful *mésalliance*. Now that he had made his point, he would withdraw his consent and put an end to this farce.

"Forasmuch as Ethan Brundy and Helen Elizabeth Charlotte Katherine Radney have consented in holy wedlock, I pronounce that they be man and wife together. In the name of the Father, and of the Son, and of the Holy Ghost. Amen."

Lady Helen's green eyes opened wide in alarm. Good God! She was married to Mr. Brundy!

The ceremony concluded, the bridal pair and their guests adjourned to the duke's residence for the wedding breakfast. Lady Helen, having put on a brave face throughout the ordeal, was inclined to think this celebration dragged on far too long, until at length it was time for her to leave her father's house for the last time. There was no wedding trip, due to the haste with which the nuptials had been arranged, and Lady Helen was not quite certain whether to be thankful that she was to be spared the forced intimacy of such a trip, or chagrined that she could not escape from Society until the gossip surrounding her shocking *mésalliance* had died down.

Suddenly she longed to sample another slice of bride cake, or to refill her glass with champagne punch — anything to postpone the inevitable departure and consequential beginning of her married life. But she was still a Radney, by blood if no longer in name, and Radneys did not shirk their duty, no matter how unpleasant that duty might be. And so, with head held high, Lady Helen Brundy accepted her husband's escort to his waiting carriage and allowed him to hand her inside.

Alone together for the first time since the brief interview which had culminated in Mr. Brundy's proposal of marriage, the newly married pair found very little to say to each other.

"I 'ope you'll be pleased with me 'ouse," Mr. Brundy said at last, breaking the silence which had reached the point of awkwardness. "On Grosvenor Square, it is. I bought it just last month, from a bloke by the name of Winslow."

"Winslow?" echoed Lady Helen, surprised out of her silence. "You cannot mean Lord Winslow, who took his own life after losing his fortune at games of chance?"

"Aye, that'll be the one," assented Mr. Brundy with a nod. "Seems 'is widow 'ad to sell it in order to pay 'is lordship's debts. Quite a bargain it was, too."

Lady Helen, it seemed, was less than pleased with her husband's business savvy. "You would seem very quick to profit from the misfortunes of others."

"'Twas not I 'oo made 'im play 'azard," Mr. Brundy pointed out reasonably. "Nor I 'oo blew the fellow's brains out."

"I suppose not," conceded Lady Helen with a sigh. "Still, it must have been very hard on Lady Winslow, to lose her husband and her home all at once."

"And 'ow would she 'ave settled the debts if no one 'ad bought the 'ouse?"

"Mr. Ethan Brundy, savior of impoverished nobility," drawled Lady Helen. "I wonder, what did you pay my father for me?"

"Seventy-five thousand pounds."

"Good heavens! You must be mad!"

"Mad?" echoed Mr. Brundy. "Why?"

"Seventy-five thousand pounds for a bride can hardly be considered a wise investment," Lady Helen pointed out.

"You'll allow me to be the best judge o' that." Mr. Brundy smiled at his bride, and there was something about the expression in his brown eyes that caused Lady Helen to look away without knowing exactly why.

"And so, like the workhouse, you paid another to take you," she concluded tartly. "It would appear you are not so very far removed from your origins, after all."

"'ere we are," said Mr. Brundy as the carriage

rolled to a stop before the imposing facade. Lady Helen's drooping spirits lifted ever so slightly. The house, with its pilastered walls and arched windows, was certainly worthy of a duke's daughter — even if she had to share it with a weaver. Why, in a house this large, she might be able to go for days without seeing her husband at all.

A footman hurried to open the carriage door, and Lady Helen, acknowledging his presence with a regal nod, allowed him to hand her down. Mr. Brundy followed, and took her arm to escort her into her new home. Inside the marble hall, all the servants were lined up to be presented to their new mistress, from Evers, the stiff-rumped butler (who looked ten times more genteel than his employer), to the lowliest scullery maid. She progressed slowly down the line as each servant bowed or curtsied a greeting, acknowledging each with a nod, sometimes speaking a word or two to those of the upper ranks.

Having grown up in the ducal household, Lady Helen was accustomed to dealing with a large staff, and so was not at all put out of countenance by the long line of humanity bobbing and bowing before her. Still, she was aware of the curious glances being leveled at her back as she made her way down the line, and had the oddest feeling that she was being paraded for their inspection as much as they were for hers. The inspection at last complete, her husband suggested that she might like a tour of the house.

"I bought it furnished, me 'aving no inclination

for decorating such a pile," he explained as he conducted his bride from room to room. "As me wife, you're welcome to furnish it as you see fit."

The furnishings, as Lady Helen soon discovered, were an unattractive mish-mash of styles, from gilded rococo in the dining room to heavy Gothic in the library, according to the caprices of the Winslow fortunes. There was even an Egyptian drawing room, with furniture whose legs were formed in the shape of crocodiles.

"Good heavens!" she cried, fingering the faded draperies. "How can you bear to live in such squalor?"

A smile touched Mr. Brundy's lips. "I've lived in far worse. But if you've a fancy to redecorate, I'll 'ave someone bring you a sample book of fabrics. Order anything you like."

"Be sure I shall," replied Lady Helen with a kindling eye.

She crossed the hall to a larger drawing room, with her husband at her heels. Here she scarcely noticed the furnishings, for a massive gilt picture frame dominated the room.

"Where is the painting?" she asked, staring at the empty frame.

"I'd thought to 'ang a picture of me wife in it," Mr. Brundy explained. "I've taken the liberty of 'iring an artist to take your likeness."

Lady Helen's lips twisted in derision. Her role, as her father had implied, was to lend respectability to her husband's wealth by giving him the appearance of gentility. Who would have guessed that she, who had spurned offers from the sons of England's noblest families, would find her destiny in lending consequence to a wealthy Cit?

"If you wish to display me like a hunting trophy, I wonder you do not simply have my head stuffed and mounted, and hang it over the mantel," she remarked disdainfully.

Mr. Brundy's lips twitched. "A novel idea, me dear, but if I did that, you'd 'ave no place to 'ang this." He reached into his inside coat pocket and withdrew a long velvet box. "Something in the way of a wedding gift," he explained.

Lady Helen opened the box and stifled a gasp. Diamonds flashed up at her, a dazzling collection of stones which sparkled in the light.

"Good heavens, Mr. Brundy," she said with remarkable calm, "are you trying to blind me, or merely to dazzle me with your wealth?"

"Me name is Ethan," he reminded her. "I'd be pleased if you'd make free with it."

Lady Helen Brundy, *née* Radney, arched a condescending eyebrow. "I wonder, *Mr. Brundy,* what makes you think pleasing you must be an object with me?"

Having seen his friend securely wed, Lord David Markham escorted Lady Randall back to her own abode in harley Street, albeit not without first offering a place in his barouche to Sir Aubrey Tabor.

"A cold day in hell, eh?" he remarked as Sir

Aubrey settled himself in the rear-facing seat. "Old Nick must be shivering in his boots today."

"Aye, and so would I be if Ethan had accepted my wager," agreed the baronet.

"A wager?" echoed Lady Randall. "What wager?"

"Aubrey was so convinced that Ethan's suit would be rejected out of hand that he offered to pay him a thousand pounds on his wedding day," Lord David explained to his fair companion. "Fortunately for him, Ethan has an aversion to gambling."

"And I'll never understand why, for if ever a man had plenty to lose, it's he," complained Sir Aubrey as Lord David's barouche bowled along Oxford Street. "Although 'tis doubtful he would lose in any case, for I vow the man is a veritable Midas. Everything he touches turns to gold!"

"Does it? I wonder," said Lord David with a thoughtful frown. "I'm beginning to think I did Ethan a disservice by sponsoring him in Society."

Sir Aubrey dismissed his friend's misgivings out of hand. "Nonsense! He'll be the better for a bit of Town bronze."

"Town bronze? Bronze-plated armor might be more to the purpose. I cannot but fear for his happiness, married to a woman who despises him. And to think that it was I who introduced them!"

"Perhaps she'll grow fond of him with time," suggested Sir Aubrey. "He may not be genteel, but Ethan is the best of good fellows. 'e'll make her a fine 'usband, 'e will!"

Lord David had to smile at the baronet's imitation of Mr. Brundy's speech, but he was still unconvinced as to the wisdom of the match. "But will she make him a fine wife? *That* is the question." He shrugged. "Ah well, I suppose he has made his own bed, and now he must lie in it."

"With Lady Helen," put in Sir Aubrey, raking long, shapely fingers through artfully disarranged chestnut locks. "Brrr!"

"At least he is well aware that Lady Helen married him for his money, and so has no illusions about true love, and happily ever after, and all that," concluded Lord David.

Emily, Lady Randall, made no contribution to the conversation, but stared fixedly at the gloved hands clasped tightly in her lap. It was not so much Mr. Brundy and Lady Helen's future that troubled her, but her own. To be sure, women of Lady Helen Radney's station rarely married for love; her own marriage to Lord Randall eight years previously, while happy enough in its way, was hardly the stuff of romantic fantasy.

But her husband had been dead for five years now and she, at seven-and-twenty, was not getting any younger. From the day she had first put off her blacks, Lord David had been most particular in his attentions, but he had spoken no word of marriage from that day to this.

She cast a furtive glance at the man by her side. While she had been wool-gathering, the conversation had taken a ribald turn. Sir Aubrey had enlarged upon his King Midas metaphor to wonder aloud what might happen that night when Mr. Brundy attempted to touch his haughty bride and, in the same vein, expressed his desire to be a fly on the wall of the bridal couple's chamber. While Lord David seemed to find his remarks amusing, they brought a crease of discontent to Emily's smooth brow.

She would be a good wife to Lord David; of that she was certain. It was sometimes said, only half in jest, that if one wished to see all of Britain's finest political minds assembled under one roof, one need not look to Whitehall, but to Lady Randall's dinner table. Given the opportunity, she would be delighted to utilize her unique gifts on Lord David's behalf.

Unfortunately, if she had entertained hopes that seeing his friend entering the bonds of holy matrimony might inspire Lord David to do likewise, these seemed doomed to disappointment.

After a late supper throughout which she and her bridegroom exchanged platitudes down the length of Lady Winslow's ridiculously ornate dining room table, Lady Helen pled fatigue and sought the sanctuary of the room which was to be her bedchamber. To be sure, there was little comfort to be found in the faded wallhangings and drab window treatments, but the apartment was large and the carved rosewood bed inviting. A fire burned cheerfully in a cleverly designed fireplace inlaid with rose-colored marble, and a door in the wall opposite led, Lady Helen supposed, to a separate dressing room.

Her abigail had arrived earlier that afternoon, bringing the first of her trunks from the duke's house, and in seeing her gowns properly bestowed in the clothespress, Lady Helen had been able to avoid her husband for most of the day. Now she dismissed the woman and, clad only in her shift, sat down at the dressing table to brush out her honey-colored hair. This enterprise, however, came to an abrupt halt when the door which she had supposed led to a dressing room opened to reveal Mr. Brundy, gorgeously arrayed in a chintz dressing gown.

"*Oh!*" shrieked Lady Helen, snatching up her discarded gown and clutching it to her chest. "Who do you think you are, sir, barging into my bedchamber unannounced?"

A gleam of amusement lit Mr. Brundy's warm brown eyes. "Why, I'm your 'usband, ma'am, and as for me barging into your bedroom, I believe it's something of a tradition on the wedding night."

Horror and understanding dawned simultaneously. She had known that Mr. Brundy married her to improve his standing in Society, but never dreamed he might presume to mingle his mongrel blood with that of eight centuries of Radneys. Lady Helen could only sputter in dismay.

"But — but I thought ours was to be a marriage in name only!"

Mr. Brundy was slightly taken aback by this revelation. "I'm sorry you 'ad the wrong impression, but such an idea never crossed me mind. I'd like to 'ave young 'uns of me own, 'elen. What good is me fortune if I've no chick nor child to in'erit when I'm gone?"

"If you are contemplating an early demise, Mr. Brundy, you might select a likely brat from the workhouse," suggested Lady Helen with something approaching her usual spirit.

"Aye, that I might," agreed Mr. Brundy with a smile. "But I'd prefer to 'ave a go at begetting me own."

Lady Helen was distressed to discover that her tart tongue failed her just when she needed it most. Mr. Brundy, finding his bride for once bereft of speech, was emboldened to place a comforting hand on her shoulder. He had long since removed the lavender gloves he had worn to the wedding, and though his hands were clean and well-manicured, they were also callused and rough. As his work-hardened fingers brushed her bare flesh, Lady Helen shuddered.

This unpromising reaction, however involuntary, was not lost on Mr. Brundy. "Under the circumstances, per'aps we'd best take some time to get to know each other before we attempt to, er, beget heirs," he suggested, allowing his hand to fall to his side.

"I — I would appreciate that," Lady Helen said haltingly, finding her voice at last.

"Very well. I shall give you six months."

"Only six?" whispered Lady Helen, clutching her flimsy shield all the tighter.

"Don't press your luck, me dear," recommended Mr. Brundy with a rueful smile. "Most men would say that I've the patience of a saint as it is, or else that I've rats in me garret." He bent and dropped a light kiss onto the top of Lady Helen's honey-colored head. "Good night, 'elen. Sleep well."

He left the room through the same door he had entered, beyond which lay a second bed-chamber, one whose furnishings were distinctly masculine. As soon as the door had closed behind him, Lady Helen leaped to her feet, snatched up a spindle-legged Sheraton chair, and wedged it securely underneath the doorknob.

In the privacy of his own room, Mr. Brundy studied the closed door which separated him from his bride. Without the outward trappings of aristocracy, she looked younger and more vulnerable, though certainly no less lovely, than she had that first night at Covent Garden. He smiled a little at the picture she had presented, with her unbound hair cascading over her shoulders and the gentle swell of her bosom behind its muslin barricade. Surely he had not been mistaken in thinking that somewhere beneath the haughty Society air lurked a vibrant young woman with a heart to be won.

And win her he would; he had come too far to fail now. He had made up his mind to wed her, and now she was his wife — in every way except that which mattered the most. Winning her hand had been almost too easy; he would have felt like a thief accepting Sir Aubrey's thousand pounds. Winning her heart, however, was likely to prove an entirely different matter. His offer of a six-month adjustment period had been as much for his own sake as hers, as it would give him time to woo his unwilling bride. In twelve hours of marriage, he had felt the sting of Lady Helen's scorn, to be sure, but he'd endured worse tongue-lashings in his life — been knocked around a bit, too, for that matter — and he had always come about in the end.

No, the Lady Helen Brundy would not be easily won, but in his experience, few things worth having were.

4

'Tis pride, rank pride, and haughtiness of soul.
          JOSEPH ADDISON, *Cato*

Early the next morning, as dawn cast its gray light over Grosvenor Square, Sukey the upstairs maid tiptoed into Lady Helen's bedchamber. The bed curtains were tightly drawn, and the sound of regular breathing within gave Sukey to understand that her ladyship was still abed and fast asleep. Quietly, so as not to disturb the slumberer, she knelt before the grate and swept out the ashes, then laid and lit a new fire with the swift efficiency of long practice.

She had performed the chore many times while her former mistress, Lady Winslow, had occupied this room. But today something seemed out of place, something so subtle that she could not say precisely what had changed. Shrugging the thought aside, she picked up the dustbin and was about to slip quietly from the room when she froze in her tracks, almost dropping the bucket of ashes in the shock of suddenly recognizing the difference in the room's arrangement.

A dainty Sheraton chair, which had previously stood against the wall flanking the dressing table, was now wedged beneath the knob of the door which connected the suite to the one adjoining.

"Gor!" breathed Sukey, momentarily forgetting the need for silence. The new mistress had locked the master out of her bedchamber, and on his wedding night, no less! Hitching the dustbin higher onto her hip, she scurried quietly past the bed and out the door, eager to share her discovery.

She found an eager audience in the downstairs maid, Annie, who sighed over her employer's plight and gave it as her opinion that he would have done far better to have wed a nice girl of his own class — someone, in fact, very much like herself.

Sukey, while in complete agreement with Annie's sentiments, took instant exception to that damsel's proposing herself as a suitable bride for the master. Indeed, so violent was her opposition that the two girls might have come to blows, had it not been for the timely intervention of Mrs. Givens, the housekeeper.

"What is going on here?" she demanded, arms akimbo in a belligerent stance as she glared at the quarreling maids. "Stop this yammering at once!"

" 'Twas she who started it!"

"Not I! *You* was the one saying as how Mr. Brundy should have married you!"

"Foolish girls!" chided Mrs. Givens, interrupting before hostilities could be resumed. "As Mr. Brundy is already married, neither of your opinions can say anything to the purpose!"

"Yes, but it could be annulled. It's un — uncommiserated," Sukey confided to her superior, and had the satisfaction of finding herself the center of that exalted woman's attention. "When I come to clean the grate just now, there was the door closed and a chair shoved under the knob, big as life. Locked him out, she did, sure as I'm standing here."

"Mark my words, Sukey, you'll not be standing here much longer if you don't learn to keep a still tongue in your head! Back to work, both of you, and no more gossiping about your betters, do you hear? If you've got something that needs saying, you come to me!"

Thus chastised, the two girls returned to their respective duties with heads hung low. Mrs. Givens waited until they were out of sight, then sought out the butler in his pantry.

"Mr. Evers, have you a moment?" she asked. "I've just heard the most *astonishing* tale!"

While Sukey's tidbit made its way through the downstairs grapevine, the news that Lady Helen Radney, daughter of His Grace, the Duke of Reddington, had been married to Mr. Ethan Brundy of Manchester the previous day in a small, private ceremony was delivered to an astonished *ton* with their breakfast trays via a discreet announcement in *The Morning Post.* The predictable result was that a crush of carriages choked Grosvenor Square as the curious flocked to gawk at the happy couple under the guise of paying their respects.

The visitors were received in the Egyptian drawing room, where Lady Helen sat (or rather, stood) for her portrait. She wore the same white and silver gown she had worn that night at Covent Garden, with one addition: about her neck was clasped the magnificent collar of diamonds her husband had given her as a wedding gift. It had been his particular request that she wear the ensemble, and since Lady Helen professed the matter to be one of supreme indifference to her, she had conceded to his wishes in this regard.

At that moment, the couple's well-wishers included the bride's brother, Viscount Tisdale, inspired no doubt by some vague notion of supporting his sister through the ordeal; Lady Randall, who had not forgotten Lord David's misgivings concerning the marriage; and sundry other denizens of the *ton* inspired by varying degrees of goodwill, curiosity, or outright malice. Among these former was the spinster Miss Maplethorpe, a lady of indeterminate age who had brought a gift for the bride. This, when opened, proved to be a packet of embroidered handkerchiefs bearing, not the crest of some noble house, but a simple letter "B" entwined with roses. However pure her intentions might have been, Miss Maplethorpe could not have selected anything more symbolic of Lady Helen's fall in Society's eyes.

"Oh!" exclaimed Lady Helen in feigned delight, too proud to show her humiliation. "You really shouldn't have, Miss Maplethorpe."

"'Twas nothing," replied the spinster modestly, blissfully unaware of the strong emotions warring within Lady Helen's breast. "I always like to do whatever I can for a new bride. I must say, Lady Helen, that your husband is —" she glanced across the room at the plebian Mr. Brundy, deep in conversation with Lady Randall, and struggled for something generous to say. "That is, er, well, he certainly is —"

"Yes, Miss Maplethorpe," agreed Lady Helen in clear, carrying tones, "he is quite fabulously wealthy."

Mr. Brundy could not possibly have failed to hear this declaration, but Lady Helen was denied the satisfaction of seeing his response by the quick-thinking Lady Randall, who chose that moment to announce, "I have decided to give a ball in honor of Mr. Brundy and Lady Helen, Miss Maplethorpe. Do say you will come!"

To Lady Randall's surprise, Mr. Brundy's face turned crimson. "You're too kind, me lady —"

"A ball?" gushed the spinster Miss Maplethorpe, oblivious to her host's discomfort. "Why, Lady Randall, what a splendid idea!"

"Splendid, indeed," agreed a new voice. "I beg you, Lady Randall, do not forget me when you make out your guest list."

Lady Helen's heart leaped into her throat as Lord Waverly entered the room with feline grace. She had been dreading his discovery of her unequal marriage more than any other. How he would mock her for marrying such a man, when she might have been his countess! And what could she say to his jibes, when he would be quite correct in his assessment?

"Lord Waverly," she said with admirable calm, holding out her hand to him.

"Mrs. Brundy," he replied with a faintly mocking smile, raising her ungloved hand to his lips. "You behold me devastated."

Her answering smile was a brittle one. "Devastated you must be, my lord, if you have forgotten how to address me. Though I am wed, I am still 'Lady Helen' to you."

"If you might lower your chin, Lady Helen," begged the artist, hard at work behind his easel.

"But of course you are still Lady Helen. How very gauche of me. Lord Waverly's gaze fell to the diamonds glittering against her *décolletage*. "You told me once you had a fancy to be gilded. It would appear you have achieved your ambition with a vengeance. I congratulate you."

Mr. Brundy, observing this exchange, conceived a violent dislike for the gentleman whose bold gaze raked his wife's bosom with detached interest. Although he vaguely recalled seeing the man in Lady Helen's box that night at Covent Garden, he could not remember having been in-

troduced. Then again, he might have been introduced to the Prince Regent himself and not remembered; he'd had eyes only for Lady Helen
Radney.

"'Oo's 'e?" asked Mr. Brundy, leaning over to
address the viscount in an undervoice.

"The Earl of Waverly. The fellow used to be
one of Nell's suitors."

Mr. Brundy had not supposed that Lady
Helen Radney would have been completely without admirers, but until now these gentlemen had
been an anonymous lot, without names or faces
to cause him undue concern. Now the bridegroom weighed his vanquished rival's elegant figure in form-fitting coat and tight pantaloons, and
found him wanting. "Why, 'e's naught but a
bloomin' fashion plate! I'll not believe 'elen
could care for such a man-milliner!"

"As to that, I couldn't say, but before Papa lost
his — that is, before you offered for her, 'twas on
the books at White's that she would have Lord
Waverly."

While Mr. Brundy digested this information,
Lord Waverly exchanged pleasantries with Lady
Randall and Miss Maplethorpe, then bethought
himself of an appointment with his tailor and
rose to take leave of his host.

"Weston, in Old Bond Street, you know," he
added by way of explanation, then raised his
quizzing glass to examine Mr. Brundy's poorly
cut morning coat. "Then again, perhaps you
don't." He shook hands with the weaver, then

wiped his hand on the tail of his coat in a gesture that was not quite surreptitious enough to go unnoticed by the bridegroom. "I congratulate you on your recent nuptials, Mr. Brundy. Your wealth has purchased you quite a prize. Your servant, sir. Lady Helen —" He took her hand and pressed an ardent kiss into her palm "— your slave."

Over the next few days, the newly married Brundys' lives settled into a routine. While Lady Helen posed for her portrait or paid and received morning calls, her husband spent his days attending to his business interests and occasionally visiting Brooks's as a guest of Lord David Markham (who fully intended to stand his friend and benefactor for membership as soon as the *ton* had sufficient time to grow accustomed to him) or White's under the auspices of his noble father-in-law.

His initial invasion of that bastion of Tory politics was not an altogether felicitous one. The duke, leading the way, handed his hat and gloves to the porter and started up the stairs, but when Mr. Brundy tried to follow, he found his way blocked by that selfsame porter.

"Oh, no you don't," said this worthy, positioning his considerable girth between the invader and the open doorway. "Members only. Now, move along!"

Mr. Brundy drew himself up to his full height. "I'm the guest of 'is Grace, the Dook," he informed the porter in lofty tones.

"And I'm the Czar of all the Russias," scoffed the doorman, unimpressed.

"You don't understand —"

"No, 'tis *you* who don't understand. Let me enlighten you."

Before the hapless Mr. Brundy knew what he was about, the porter had seized him by the collar and would have thrown him bodily into the street, had the duke not become aware of the fracas behind him and turned on the stairs.

"For God's sake, man, the fellow is my son-in-law! Let him go!"

"Y-Yes, your Grace! At once, your Grace!"

Thus chastised, the porter not only unhanded Mr. Brundy, but went so far as to try to repair the damage to his coat and cravat. Mr. Brundy, unable to resist the temptation, cast a pitying smile on the groveling doorman before climbing the stairs in the duke's wake.

"Now, remember," the duke instructed his son-in-law, "all the gentlemen you are about to meet are staunch Tories."

"I'll try not to 'old it against them, your Grace," promised Mr. Brundy.

This earned him a glare from his papa-in-law. "On no account are you to argue politics with any of them! Just nod your head and keep your mouth shut. And do try not to look so common!"

Perhaps Mr. Brundy was trying so hard to determine how he might carry out this last command that he quite forgot the other two. At any rate, when he heard three of his new acquaintances discussing a speech made the day before in the House of Lords, Mr. Brundy moved his chair nearer so that he might catch every word.

"— Poundstone is exactly right when he says it would mean economic disaster," Lord Chester was saying. "A tradesman can acquire an apprentice from the workhouse for a fraction of what it would cost him to hire a grown man to do the same job."

Lord Hewett nodded. "Besides driving up prices, think of all the children who would be thrown onto the parish, contributing nothing to their own upkeep, but costing more than ever to feed and clothe —"

"And once they're grown, the brats will breed like rabbits, and then there will be even more of them," put in Lord Ravenwood.

Mr. Brundy tensed, but said nothing.

"All eating their heads off and requiring even higher taxes to support them," seconded Chester. "No, the workhouse system may not be perfect, but it is surely the best alternative."

Mr. Brundy had sincerely tried to obey his father-in-law's behests, but at last he could hold his tongue no longer. "I wonder if the 'brats' would agree," he remarked, and although he had not raised his voice, he instantly had the three men's undivided attention.

"In all likelihood they would not," conceded Hewett. "But when did children ever know what was best for them?"

"That is why we, as men, must decide these

things," agreed Lord Chester. Seeing his primary audience was unconvinced, he added, "No one likes to see young children put to work, Mr. Brundy, but 'tis a necessary evil."

"Tell me, gentlemen, 'ave you any children of your own?"

The childless lords Hewett and Ravenwood looked mildly annoyed at the abrupt change of subject, but Lord Chester fairly beamed with paternal pride. "Indeed, I have, sir. Three fine sons and two lovely daughters."

"And would you, for any reason, think it in their best interests to be chained to a piece of machinery for upwards of twelve hours a day?"

The duke had wandered to the far side of the room to speak to his cronies, and had been involved in lively debate over the merits of Sir Arnold Longacre's thoroughbred racehorse when his son-in-law's unrefined accents caught his attention — along, it seemed, with that of every other gentleman in the room. Following the sound, he discovered Mr. Brundy waxing eloquent on the subject of labor reform to an enthralled audience, while Lord Chester, his face quite purple, looked on the verge of an apoplexy.

" 'Chained', Mr. Brundy?" scoffed Lord Ravenwood. "Surely not!"

Mr. Brundy shrugged. "And 'ow else would you keep a 'ealthy young lad at 'is post for that length of time?"

"If I may say so, sir, you seem remarkably well-informed — to say nothing of passionate — on the subject," put in a new voice.

"Indeed I am, on both counts. I was one of those brats, you see," Mr. Brundy informed the newcomer, a man whose pleasant countenance was framed by bushy blond sidewhiskers just beginning to show traces of silver. Although only in his mid-forties, he walked with a pronounced limp, yet his bearing still bespoke the soldier in spite of his disability.

"Well, then," blustered Lord Chester, recovering his poise. "You came through the current system, and you seem to have done quite well for yourself. A wealthy man, married to one of the most fêted women in England —"

"Aye, that I am," agreed Mr. Brundy, his expression softening at the thought of his beautiful bride. "I guess I'm luckier than most."

"Speaking of luck, let us see if yours extends to whist," barked his Grace, seizing the opportunity to remove his errant son-in-law to the card room.

"Thanks, but I'm not a betting man," replied Mr. Brundy. "If you've no objection, I'll wait 'ere and 'ave a look at the *Times* until you've finished."

The duke regarded his son-in-law with a darkening brow. "Tell me, Mr. Brundy, are you a Methodist?"

"That I'm not, your Grace, but I've no wish to toss away me 'ard earned money at cards."

Muttering imprecations against the moral posturings of the middling classes, the duke betook himself to the card room. The others drifted off

in his wake, sensing that the afternoon's enter-
tainment was at an end. Mr. Brundy, left to his
own devices, asked a passing waiter if he might
have a look at the famous betting book, and upon
its being delivered to him, leafed through its
pages with interest. Just as the viscount had said,
a Lord Scarsdale had wagered £200 against a
Captain Sir Charles Fortescue's chestnut gelding
that Lady Helen Radney would marry Lord
Waverly, while numerous side bets speculated as
to the date of the union. He did not know any
Lord Scarsdale, nor could he recall meeting a
Captain Sir Charles Fortescue, but he noted with
satisfaction that his lordship had paid the debt in
full on Friday, 25 April 1816 — the date the announcement of his own marriage to Lady Helen
had appeared in *The Morning Post.*

He closed the book with a much lighter heart,
then made his way to the card room to follow the
duke's progress at whist.

While her husband debated politics at White's,
Lady Helen weighed the merits of curtains ver-
sus cornices, and reupholstering the existing furnishings as opposed to purchasing new ones.
Indeed, she took so much pleasure in this house-
wifely exercise that she was very nearly able to
forget the husband whose largesse made it all
possible. True to his word, Mr. Brundy had
arranged for a clerk to call on his wife with a
book of fabric samples.

"I do like this polished cotton for the drawing

room windows," she said, fingering a sample of blue and coral birds of paradise on a cream background. "The pattern is quite unique, and the workmanship obviously superior."

"Some say the finest in England, ma'am," said the little man, fairly puffing out his chest with pride.

"The yellow floral would look well enough in my bedchamber," Lady Helen continued, "but on the whole I think I prefer the striped rose pattern."

"If I may say so, your ladyship has an unerring eye," applauded the clerk, jotting down her selections in a small notepad. "And what do you favor for the gentleman's suite? Might I suggest this green jacquard?"

In almost a week of marriage, Lady Helen had never set foot inside her husband's bedroom, and she felt the heat rise to her face at the mention of that forbidding and mysterious territory. "Yes, well, as to that, I — I think I have spent quite enough for one day," she stammered, seizing upon the excuse provided by the ever-lengthening list. "You may present the bill to my husband, Mr. Wetherstone."

The look he gave her was a puzzled blank. "The bill, my lady?"

"For the fabrics. Or would you prefer payment upon delivery?"

Enlightenment dawned, and Mr. Wetherstone permitted himself a smile at her innocent question. "There is no charge, my lady. I will simply have the necessary lengths sent over from your husband's warehouses."

Now it was Lady Helen's turn to be confused. "From my husband's — ? Mr. Wetherstone, are you saying that *Mr. Brundy's mill* produced all these fabrics?"

"All these and more, my lady."

"Well — well, why did you not say so?" she demanded, feeling incredibly foolish.

"Begging your pardon, my lady, but I thought you knew," said the clerk apologetically.

Lady Helen had no intention of turning her home, purchased as it was with her freedom, into an advertisement for her husband's business. For a moment she considered punishing him by cancelling the order and purchasing textiles imported from the Continent at exorbitant expense. Then she thought of the bird of paradise print she had chosen for the drawing room. It truly was lovely, and she would never find anything like it, at any price. It would be foolish, she decided, to cut off her nose merely to spite her face. With some misgivings, she let the order stand.

Her husband, however, she had no intention of letting off so lightly. Upon his return, she greeted him with honeyed sweetness (a circumstance which in itself warned him that all was not well within the Brundy domicile) and asked him if he had passed a pleasant afternoon at White's.

"I don't know as 'ow I'd call it pleasant," Mr. Brundy answered with great deliberation, "but they won't be forgetting me any time soon. I'm in the suds with your papa, me dear, and no mistake."

"What did you do?" asked Lady Helen with a growing sense of unease.

The look he gave her was all innocence. "Why, I only expressed me honest opinion," he insisted.

"If we are to speak of honesty," Lady Helen said tartly, seeing her opening, "you might have told me that those were your own samples you sent for!"

"You knew I owned a mill, 'elen. Did you think it produced nothing but 'omespun?"

This rhetorical question was far closer to the truth than Lady Helen cared to admit.

"On the contrary, Mr. Brundy, I have never felt the matter worthy of serious consideration," she replied haughtily.

Mr. Brundy only grinned at her. Really, she thought, the man was impervious to insult! Any of her London beaux would have turned tail and run to lick their wounds. What could one do with a man who merely smiled at one in a way that made one feel suddenly hot and cold all at the same time?

"I have decided to keep the furniture in the large drawing room and simply have it reupholstered," Lady Helen said hastily, more out of a need to fill the lengthening silence than any desire to inform her husband of the changes in store. "I'm also keeping my bed and dressing table, and recovering the Sheraton chairs in my bedroom." This remark was unfortunate, as it brought to mind the chair wedged beneath the doorknob, and Lady Helen lapsed into blushing silence.

But if Mr. Brundy noticed his wife's discomfiture, he gave no outward sign. "And what of the pieces you don't wish to keep?" he asked. "'ave you decided what to do with them?"

"I haven't the faintest idea," confessed Lady Helen. "I might let the housekeeper have a couple of the chairs for her room, but I hardly think she would want those dreadful Egyptian crocodiles crawling about the place."

"Might I make a suggestion?"

"I would love to hear it," declared Lady Helen, although there was that in her voice which indicated otherwise.

"I thought per'aps we might write Lady Winslow and see if she might wish to 'ave any pieces she was particularly fond of."

Lady Helen blinked at her base-born husband in surprise. "I think that would be a very decent thing to do, Mr. Brundy."

"I may not be genteel, 'elen, but I am — decent — on occasion," he pointed out gently.

Remembering her six-month reprieve from her conjugal duties, Lady Helen could not deny it.

5

Chaste to her husband, frank to all beside.
ALEXANDER POPE, *Moral Essays*

If the newly married Brundys were able to fill their days with meaningful activity, the same could not be said of their nights. While the *ton* might avail itself of the upstart weaver's hospitality in order to satisfy its curiosity, inviting the creature into their own homes was quite another matter. Consequently, the weaver and his wife spent their evenings quietly at home, facing one another down the long expanse of the new mahogany dining table. To Lady Helen, accustomed as she was to choosing between three or more invitations on any given night, this forced isolation was rather difficult to bear, even though she was not entirely without sympathy for the London hostesses who had crossed her off their guest lists.

Ironically, it was ultimately Mr. Brundy to whom she owed her deliverance. For among the witnesses to his debut at White's, and thus privy to that shocking display of insubordination to his

74

betters which had so mortified the duke, was one Colonel Lionel Pickering.

The Colonel had distinguished himself on the field of battle some twenty years earlier, until a ball in the knee had abruptly ended his military career and left him with a permanent limp. His disability notwithstanding, Pickering had still managed to win the heart and hand of plump, pretty Elizabeth Collins, who had rewarded his heroism by presenting him with no less than four bright-eyed daughters. The eldest of the Misses Pickering was making her come-out that very Season, and it was largely to escape the endless details of her presentation ball that Col. Pickering had sought refuge at his club on that particular day.

He had returned to his domicile to find his wife fretting over the invitation list and wondering aloud how much champagne would be necessary to quench their guests' thirst, how many lobster patties to satiate their hunger, and how many wax candles to illuminate their finery without setting them ablaze.

"I do hope you will not be bored, my dear," she clucked, glancing at her husband's cane. "It must be perfectly dreadful, hosting a ball when one cannot dance."

"Nonsense," her spouse replied briskly. "Have I ever refused to escort you or Amanda to Almack's?"

This comparison found no favor with Mrs. Pickering. "No, but you always abandon us for the card room the minute you are inside the door. Here you are the host, so I shall tolerate no disappearances!"

"Very well. Only promise me you will invite plenty of interesting people with whom I may converse."

"You have my word," vowed Mrs. Pickering. "Did you have anyone particular in mind?"

"As a matter of fact, I met a man just today whom I should like to know better. Have you perhaps heard of a Mr. Ethan Brundy, of Manchester?"

Mrs. Pickering's brown eyes bulged. "Brundy? Is he not the weaver who married the duke of Reddington's daughter?"

"The very same. Mr. Brundy was at White's today as the duke's guest. His opinions, though not eloquently expressed, were most thought-provoking. I should like you to send a card to Mr. Ethan Brundy and Lady Helen Brundy."

"Are you quite sure, dearest?" fretted his wife. "I should not wish to do anything to damage Amanda's chances. We do have the other three girls to think of, you know."

"I yield to your superior social sense," conceded the Colonel meekly, bowing his head to hide the smile he could not quite suppress. "I am sure we want Amanda's come-out ball to be a dignified occasion, not fodder for drawing-room gossip."

Mrs. Pickering regarded her husband with an arrested expression. "Gossip, my love?"

"I fear it would be the talk of the *ton* for at least a week — particularly if you were also to invite Lord Waverly. He was expected to wed Lady Helen himself, you know. No, if the word were to get out that the Brundys had been invited, we should no doubt find ourselves besieged by every gabble-grinder in London. You are right as always, Liza, my dear."

Having made his point, the Colonel beat a strategic retreat, leaving his wife's head fairly spinning as she considered the possibilities. The talk of the *ton* for at least a week . . . every gabble-grinder in London . . . who would be escorted to the ball by their marriageable sons, grandsons, and nephews, no doubt, and who then would be obliged to invite dear Amanda to their own parties. . . . Mrs. Pickering snatched up her guest list, and added three more names to the bottom.

The very next day found a folded and sealed missive on cream-colored vellum delivered to Lady Helen Brundy with the morning post. Since this of late had consisted mostly of letters from various ducal relations offering felicitations to her upon her marriage, while tendering the most tortured explanations as to why they were regrettably unable to offer hospitality to the bridal couple, Lady Helen seized upon this promising correspondence with the greed of a child being offered a sweetmeat. Upon breaking the seal and spreading open the single sheet, she was informed that the pleasure of her company was requested at a ball in honor of Miss Amanda Pickering's introduction to Society. Unfortunately, Mr. Brundy's presence was requested as well, but Lady Helen was weary enough of her own company that a ball, even one to which her husband was invited, was a welcome diversion.

"We have been invited to a ball, Mr. Brundy, and I plan to attend," she informed him that evening over the dinner table. "Shall I add your name to my acceptance?"

"If it's all the same to you, me dear, I prefer to stay 'ome," he said. "I've no fondness for balls and such like."

Lady Helen, who just that morning would have been delighted at the prospect of attending the ball without the encumbrance of her lowborn spouse, was chagrined at how unsatisfactory she found his answer. "As you wish," she said, shrugging her slender shoulders. "Still, I would have thought you would be bored with your own company by now."

"With me own company, per'aps," he nodded. "But when a man is wed to one of the cleverest and most beautiful women in England, why should 'e look outside 'is own 'ome for amusement?"

Lady Helen was annoyed to feel her face grow warm. "Sarcasm does not become you, Mr. Brundy."

"Perfectly honest, me dear. But if you wish to go, I'll not forbid you."

"I do. I've no doubt Papa would escort me, or Teddy. Or," she added, prompted by some demon she could not name, "perhaps Lord Waverly could be persuaded."

If she had wished to goad her husband into some show of jealousy, she succeeded admirably. Mr. Brundy's fork clattered to his plate, and his usually good-humored countenance darkened ominously. "Lord Waverly, you say?"

"Why, yes. When one is a married woman, one need not be so particular as to the proprieties, you know. 'Tis not unusual among the *ton* for a matron to be escorted by a man other than her husband."

"We've a word for that sort of thing in Lancashire," muttered Mr. Brundy, unimpressed.

Raising one delicately arched eyebrow, Lady Helen regarded him haughtily from the other end of the long table. "You are not in Lancashire, Mr. Brundy."

"Nevertheless, if you want go to Mrs. What's-'er-name's ball, you'll go with your 'usband. You may write and tell 'er we'll be 'appy to attend."

"I shall, of course, be pleased to accept your escort," replied Lady Helen with crushing formality.

It was not until later, as she penned her acceptance, that she wondered why she had not left well enough alone.

And so it was that Mr. Brundy and Lady

Helen made their first public appearance as man and wife. Lady Helen was, as ever, breathtaking in gold sarcenet shot with threads of metallic gold, in direct defiance of the tabbies who would no doubt be whispering behind their fans that poor Lady Helen Radney was the latest vestal virgin to be sacrificed on the altar of that most precious of metals.

But when she descended the stairs to find her husband there before her, her defiant spirit withered and died. Indeed, the sight of his ill-fitting evening clothes and unkempt dark curls made her wonder anew why she had not been content to solicit her brother's escort and leave her husband at home. Alas, the carriage was even now at the door, and it was too late to change her plans. She allowed Evers to place her velvet evening cloak about her shoulders, then took Mr. Brundy's proffered arm.

After a short carriage drive, the Brundys reached Portland Place, where Colonel Pickering had hired a house for the Season. A long line of vehicles formed a queue which snaked up the street, each carriage in turn disgorging its glittering occupants before the front door.

"It appears Miss Pickering's come-out ball is destined to be quite a crush," observed Lady Helen to her spouse.

"Indeed, it does," he agreed.

There was little more to be said after that, and so the pair waited in silence while their carriage edged ever closer to its destination. This at last having been reached, the carriage door was thrown open and a liveried footman assisted Lady Helen from the vehicle.

As Mr. Brundy escorted his wife up the stairs to the first-floor ballroom, Lady Helen noted with satisfaction the polished parquet floors, sparkling crystal chandeliers, and huge bowls of flowers atop pedestals made to resemble classical Greek columns. It was good to be out in Society again, to resume her place in the world to which she had been born and bred — the world to which her husband, in spite of his wealth, could never truly belong. With a disdainful sniff, she released his arm and disappeared into the cloak room to divest herself of her velvet cloak. Great was her surprise when she emerged to find her husband being hailed with enthusiasm by their host.

"Well met, Mr. Brundy!" exclaimed Colonel Pickering, clapping him on the back as he might an intimate of long standing. "Where have you been keeping yourself? Haven't seen you at White's this age."

"No, nor will you." Mr. Brundy's brown eyes twinkled. "The Dook threatened to 'ave me 'orsewhipped if I dared show me face there again."

The Colonel guffawed, drawing curious glances in their direction from the other guests. "Did he, now? Then I fear you are doomed either way, my friend, for I shall have you horsewhipped if you do not! White's is a duller place without you, Brundy."

"Why, thank you, sir. What a 'andsome way of saying I made a spectacle of meself!"

"A most welcome one, I assure you. Do you know, I have just read a most thought-provoking treatise by Mrs. More on the subject of education for the lower classes. I should be most interested in hearing your opinion of it." The colonel paused awkwardly, then asked, "You do read, do you not?"

Mr. Brundy nodded. "Although I 'aven't the advantage of an Oxford education, I am not completely illiterate, Colonel."

"No, no, of course not," muttered Colonel Pickering, embarrassed at his own *faux pas*. "No offense intended, I assure you."

"And none taken," replied Mr. Brundy, grinning broadly. "I'd be more than 'appy to see what Mrs. More 'as to say.

"Capital! The pamphlet is in my study, if you will follow me."

"Of course. If you'll excuse me, 'elen, me dear."

And to her chagrin, Lady Helen for the first time in her life found herself completely *sans* male companionship. She was still shooting dagger-glances at her husband's rapidly retreating back when a familiar drawl interrupted thoughts which were hardly shining examples of wifely submission.

"Poor Mrs. Brundy! Has the weaver tired of you so quickly?"

Turning to answer the challenge, Lady Helen

was forced to pause in order to catch her breath. After almost two weeks in the company of the badly tailored Mr. Brundy, the sight of Lord Waverly in full evening dress was indeed awe-inspiring. White pantaloons were molded to his well-muscled legs, and his dark cutaway coat caressed his broad shoulders like a lover. Nor could any fault be found with his dove gray waistcoat or pristine cravat. Indeed, the only thing marring this pattern-card of British man-hood was the fact that Lord Waverly was per-fectly well aware of the picture he presented. Fortunately, Lady Helen's tongue had not grown dull since her marriage, as she had taken every opportunity to sharpen it on her husband.

"Lord Waverly." Lady Helen acknowledged his presence with a regal nod. "I was under the im-pression that you considered balls a deadly bore. What brings you here? Are you dancing atten-dance on Miss Pickering, or have they stopped taking your vouchers at White's?"

Waverly bared his straight white teeth in a grin, but the steely look in his eyes told her she had struck too close to the mark for the earl's com-fort.

"As you have no doubt deduced, I am up the River Tick," he confessed. "But at least you need not fear a similar fate, my dear, I understand your husband is a paragon of virtue. He neither gambles nor takes snuff, but spends each day from dawn to dusk in the noble pursuit of Mammon — unless, of course, he is favoring the membership of White's with his enlightened views on the governing of the Empire."

Lady Helen unfurled her spangled Chinese fan and raised it to her mouth to hide a yawn — a gesture which somehow called attention to her ennui rather than concealing it. Lord Waverly knew her well enough to recognize a deliberate set-down when he saw one, and grinned appreciatively.

"But I should never dream of boring you. May I hope that, in the absence of your husband, you will condescend to accept your humble servant as a suitable partner for the quadrille which is about to begin?"

"Since Mr. Brundy's virtues thankfully do not extend to sitting in his wife's pocket, I should be pleased to accept your generous offer," replied Lady Helen, and allowed the earl to escort her onto the floor.

Once it became known that Lady Helen was back in circulation, and with no sign of her husband in sight, she found herself much in demand. All her former suitors came flocking back to be abused by her waspish tongue, and she had the satisfaction of seeing Captain Wentworth and Sir Toby Granger-Hughes almost come to fisticuffs over the privilege of leading her in to supper.

Her return to favor did not go unremarked by Emily, Lady Randall, who observed with a furrowed brow Lady Helen's re-emergence.

"Really, David, I cannot but think it shabby of

Mr. Brundy to neglect his wife so," she remarked to her cicisbeo when the figures of the quadrille brought them together long enough to converse.

"Nonsense, my dear," scoffed Lord David. "Most of the married couples here hardly dance together at all. 'Tis one of the strongest arguments a lady might make for remaining single," he added with a charming smile.

Indeed, one of the *only* such arguments, she wanted to say, but refrained. "But they have been married less than two weeks," she pointed out. "Surely matters have not reached such a pass in so short a time."

"Emily, how old were you when you learned to dance?"

She blinked, taken aback by the seeming *non sequitur.* "I don't recall. My governess taught me a few simple steps when I was nine or ten, so that I might join in the Sir Roger de Coverley at Christmas, and then Mama hired a dancing master for me when I was sixteen, the year before I came out."

"When Mr. Brundy was nine, he was taken from the workhouse and chained to a power loom twelve hours a day," Lord David informed her bluntly. "By the time he was sixteen, he was being groomed to take over the business."

Emily's dark eyes widened in sudden understanding. "Then — ?"

Lord David nodded. "Precisely. He never learned to dance. And though he takes a perverse sort of pride in his humble origins, he is surprisingly self-conscious about his lack of social graces. Shed no tears for Lady Helen, my dear. She accomplished a major *coup* in getting him here tonight at all. But if you wish it, I shall run the negligent bridegroom to earth."

"No, no, do not embarrass him on my account," Emily protested, but Lord David had already taken himself off in search of his friend.

He located his quarry in the library, where Mr. Brundy and Colonel Pickering were in the midst of a lively debate.

"— I can't 'elp but notice, Colonel, that while Mrs. More is all for improving the moral character of the poor, she has little to say about raising their economic status."

"I believe Mrs. More feels the poor should learn to be satisfied with their station in life," replied the colonel.

Mr. Brundy nodded. "I suspect most of the Quality would agree — provided that none of *them* should 'ave to occupy that particular station."

"*Touché*, my friend," laughed Colonel Pickering. "May I quote you on that?"

"If you wish, but I've a feeling it won't win you many friends at White's."

"No matter. The Old Guard needs shaking up every now and then, and you're just the man to do it." The colonel paused, struck by sudden inspiration. "I say, Brundy, have you ever thought of standing for Parliament?"

"Don't give him any ideas," protested Lord

David, choosing that moment to make his presence known. "If he were to challenge me, he just might win."

"Come in and have a drop of brandy with us, Lord David," exclaimed his host, but as he reached for the open bottle, his welcoming expression turned wary. "Don't tell me my wife has noticed my absence and sent you to fetch me!"

"Not at all," Lord David assured him. "I come on behalf of Ethan's wife, not yours."

The book on Mr. Brundy's lap fell to the floor as he rose to his feet. "'elen? Why? What's the matter?"

"Emily is convinced you are neglecting Lady Helen shamelessly. I, on the other hand, think she is enjoying herself far more than is proper for a bride of two weeks. She hasn't sat out a dance since Lord Waverly stood up with her for the quadrille."

Mrs. More and her theories forgotten, Mr. Brundy set his glass down with a thud and made his excuses to his host, then set his feet in the direction of the ballroom. He reached his destination while a waltz was in progress, and thus discovered Lord Waverly clasping Lady Helen in an embrace more intimate than any her own husband had as yet enjoyed. They made a very pretty picture as they whirled about the floor with practiced grace, both tall, slender, and elegantly costumed, but Mr. Brundy, waiting impatiently along the wall, took no pleasure in the sight. He might have been much heartened to know that, even as she smiled up at her partner, Lady Helen was covertly scanning the crowd for the one face noticeably absent amongst the crush.

At last the lilting strains of the violins came to a halt, and Lord Waverly led Lady Helen back to her chair, where her next partner, Sir Toby Granger-Hughes, was waiting to claim her. No sooner had she laid her hand on Sir Toby's arm than it was snatched away by her husband, who drew it firmly through the crook of his elbow.

"Time to go, me dear," he said in a voice which brooked no argument. "Gentlemen, I bid you good night."

Lady Helen held her tongue with an effort while they collected their cloaks and quit the glittering house for the gaslit street.

"Pray tell me, Mr. Brundy, just what do you think you are about?" she demanded, fairly quivering in outrage.

"I consider meself a reasonable man, 'elen, and you will find me a tolerant — nay, even an indulgent! — 'usband, but I'll not stand idly by while me wife makes me the laughingstock of London," he informed her roundly.

"You don't do yourself justice, Mr. Brundy," she replied sweetly. "You were the laughingstock of London long before you married me."

The drive back to Grosvenor Square could not be deemed a congenial one, Lady Helen being sunk in what, in a lesser female, would have been called a pout. She dared not voice her grievances, however, or the oaf beside her might think she had *wished* him to sit in her pocket all the evening long. Nothing could be further from the truth, of course, but there was a wide gulf between sitting in her pocket and spurning her company altogether. Did this vulgarian not know that he was supposed to dance attendance on her so that *she* might spurn *him?*

Of course he did not. One of the most galling aspects of this unequal marriage was the fact that Mr. Brundy failed to recognize its inequality, or if he recognized it, certainly failed to acknowledge her superior status. Yes, it was high time Mr. Ethan Brundy of Manchester was made aware of the inferiority of his position — and she, Lady Helen Brundy *née* Radney, knew just how to put him in his place.

6

The force of his own merit makes his way.
WILLIAM SHAKESPEARE,
King Henry the Eighth

While his wife plotted his downfall, Mr. Brundy, all unknowing, called in Harley Street and sent his card up to Emily, Lady Randall. Within minutes, her ladyship's butler returned to request that he wait upon her in the green saloon. Mr. Brundy was duly ushered to this chamber, where he took a seat on a striped satin chair and mentally rehearsed his speech while he awaited her ladyship's pleasure. He was relieved that she was willing to receive him at all, for although he had seen her often enough in Lord David's company, his own acquaintance with her could hardly be called intimate. Still, he needed a lady's assistance, and he was more nearly acquainted with Lady Randall than with any other lady in London, with the arguable exception of his wife. He was not at all certain as to the propriety of such a visit, but if, as Lady Helen had insisted, it was acceptable for married women to be squired about by gentlemen other than their husbands, then surely calling upon a widow, even a young and pretty one, in broad daylight could not be so heinous a crime. At any rate, he had not long to debate the matter before Emily wafted into the room in a cloud of lavender jaconet muslin.

"Mr. Brundy, an unexpected pleasure," she said, gliding toward him with both hands out-stretched. "Does your wife not accompany you?"

"Er, no," replied Mr. Brundy as he rose to bow over her hands.

"Do sit down," she urged, sinking gracefully onto the sofa opposite. "David left but moments ago. He will be sorry he missed you."

"I'm afraid I can't share 'is regrets, me lady," Mr. Brundy confessed. "To own the truth, I 'ad 'opes of seeing you alone to discuss, er, business of a personal nature."

"Indeed?" Emily remembered Lord David's misgivings about his friend's marriage, and her hackles rose. She did not know Mr. Brundy well, but she liked him enough to wish him happy in his marriage — particularly since his unhappiness would make Lord David doubly wary of that blessed institution.

Mr. Brundy cleared his throat and took a deep breath. "Lady Randall, I wonder if you would be so obliging as to teach me 'ow to dance?"

Emily, having learned a small part of Mr. Brundy's past from Lord David, found something so poignant in the simple request that her sympathies were instantly aroused. Still, one did not learn the complex figures of the quadrille in a day.

"I should certainly be willing to try, Mr. Brundy," she began cautiously, "but you must be aware that some of the more difficult steps may take months to master."

"Then I guess we'd best get started right away, 'adn't we?" replied Mr. Brundy, much cheered.

Such enthusiasm proved too contagious to resist, and Lady Randall soon found herself caught up in the spirit of the enterprise. Deeming the green saloon too small for their purposes, she led him to the music room at the rear of the house, and here they took their positions in the center of the floor.

"It is a great pity we have no one to play the pianoforte for us, but we shall do just as well by counting aloud. You stand here, Mr. Brundy, and I, as your partner, will stand here," she instructed him. "Take my hand like so, and step forward and back, forward and back. Very good! Now, reverse."

Mr. Brundy obediently followed her instructions, but as they remained a proper arm's length apart at all times, he was at last moved to mutter, "*They* weren't doing it like this."

"'They,' Mr. Brundy?"

"'elen and Waverly."

Enlightenment dawned in Emily's dark eyes. She, too, had seen Lady Helen waltzing with Lord Waverly, and thought how elegant the earl had appeared, clasping his tall and slender partner in his arms — a far cry indeed from the man Lady Helen had married. What she had not known was that Mr. Brundy had also been watching — and that he was very much in love with his wife. Emily, reflecting wistfully that Lord David had never shown the least sign of jealousy at seeing her waltz with other men, could not but be moved.

"You must be referring to the waltz," Emily said gently. "Would you like to learn how?"

"If any man is going to 'old me wife in such a way," he said with great deliberation, "it's going to be me."

"'Tis quite simple, really. Take my right hand with your left, and place your right hand at my waist."

"I — I can't," protested her embarrassed partner, taking an awkward step backwards.

"Of course you can, Mr. Brundy! People do it all the time."

"But David —"

"David will not object, believe me," Emily said with a hint of regret. "Just pretend I am Lady Helen. You do want to waltz with her, do you not?"

His resolution thus fortified, Mr. Brundy took his partner in a stiff embrace.

"That's the way," she said approvingly. "Now, begin: *one,* two, three, *one,* two, three — very good, Mr. Brundy! We shall have you waltzing at Almack's in no time."

"Almack's?" echoed Mr. Brundy, careful not to lose his count.

"Almack's Assembly Rooms, on King Street," Emily explained. "A very select establishment where one may go of a Wednesday night for dancing or cards."

"Does 'elen go there?"

"Before her marriage, she could be seen there almost every week."

Mr. Brundy, minding his steps, merely nodded. In all likelihood, last night had not been the first time Lord Waverly had held Lady Helen in an intimate embrace. Nor might it be the last, either, but from here on out, the earl would no longer have a clear field. He, Ethan Brundy, had not conquered the workhouse only to be bested on the ballroom floor.

"Ouch!" cried Emily, as her partner trod squarely upon her foot.

"I beg your pardon," protested an apologetic Mr. Brundy. "I can't think 'ow that 'appened."

"I daresay you are growing tired," suggested Emily. "Perhaps we had best save the next lesson for another day."

Mr. Brundy, not wishing to wear out his welcome, consented to this plan and took his leave of his hostess, who admonished him to practice at home and to return for further instruction whenever he wished.

"I'll do that, me lady," he assured her. "Oh, and one more thing. I'd be grateful if you wouldn't mention this to David, at least not yet."

"Your secret is safe with me, Mr. Brundy." *Both of them*, she promised herself.

After successfully completing his first dance lesson, Mr. Brundy was content to spend the evening quietly at home. He had promised Colonel Pickering that he would read Mrs. More's tome in its entirety before passing final judgement upon it, and it was with the intention of retrieving the book from his study that he was crossing the marble-tiled hall when a sound from above drew his gaze upwards.

The sight which met his eyes fairly took his breath away. Lady Helen descended the stairs in a cloud of silk gauze whose willow green shade exactly matched her eyes. Her honey-blond hair was dressed simply and ornamented with a single white gardenia over her left ear. Mr. Brundy, normally the most pragmatic of men, was struck with the fanciful notion that she resembled an exotic hothouse flower — a poetic observation which was immediately supplanted by the recollection of his own far more casual attire.

"I say, 'elen, 'ave we an engagement I've forgotten?" he asked, taking up a position beside the newel post so that he might hand her down the last few stairs.

Lady Helen gave him her hand, along with a look of wide-eyed innocence. "Why, no, Mr. Brundy. I am merely going to Almack's. 'Tis Wednesday, you know."

"Indeed, it is," he said with a secretive smile.

"Still, I trust you're not going alone."

"No, indeed." Lady Helen's rebuttal was interrupted by a knock upon the front door. "That must be my escort now," she said, smiling brightly at her husband.

Evers answered the summons and stepped back to admit Lord Waverly, immaculate as ever in full evening dress.

"Ah, Lady Helen, you are a vision, as always," he said, raising her gloved hands to his lips before turning startled eyes upon her husband. "But what is this? Do you not mean to accompany us, Mr. Brundy?"

"Mr. Brundy is looking forward to a quiet evening at home," explained Lady Helen.

"A wise choice, Mr. Brundy, I feel sure," said the earl, nodding his approval. "Lady Helen, shall we go?"

Evers stepped forward with his mistress's evening cloak but, seeing Mr. Brundy hold out an imperative hand, surrendered it to his master instead. Mr. Brundy placed the velvet garment about his wife's shoulders, allowing his hands to remain there the merest fraction of a second longer than was absolutely necessary. This proprietary gesture did not go unremarked by Lord Waverly, who acknowledged it with the slightest lift of an eyebrow before offering his arm to Lady Helen.

"I 'ope you 'ave a pleasant evening, me dear." Mr. Brundy's unrefined accents followed them to the front door.

"Thank you, Mr. Brundy. I'm sure I shall."

Once outside, Lady Helen allowed herself to be handed into Lord Waverly's carriage, her spirits somewhat dashed. She was on her way to Almack's, the one place in all of London to which all Mr. Brundy's wealth could not buy him entrée. Furthermore, she was going there in the company of no less a personage than the Earl of Waverly, a man whom, had circumstances not decreed otherwise, she might have married. Her husband should have been beside himself, but instead he merely wished that she might have a pleasant evening.

In the twenty-four hours since the Pickerings' ball, she had had ample time to reflect on Mr. Brundy's treatment of her, and her response to it. True, he had ignored her shamefully, but even more disturbing was the fact that she had been so bothered by his neglect. The man was a *weaver,* for heaven's sake! His attentions would have been an embarrassment which she was thankful to have been spared. More disturbing than all was the recollection of that moment when he had practically snatched her out of her partner's arms, and the mortifying discovery that she had been trying to provoke this reaction from the moment she had first allowed the earl to escort her onto the floor.

In the light of these alarming revelations, it was perhaps not surprising that a pall had been cast over her evening which even the exclusive company at Almack's did little to lift. Her companion, noting her uncharacteristic reserve, plied her with cakes and lemonade and, at the first available opportunity, waltzed her into a secluded alcove.

"Alone at last," he said, without releasing his hold on her.

Lady Helen firmly disengaged herself from his embrace. "You seem to forget, my lord, that I am a married woman."

"On the contrary, no one is more acutely aware of that fact than I, excepting, perhaps, your esteemed husband. And your marriage, as you must know, changes everything."

This, certainly, was no lie. Three weeks ago, she would have never have concerned herself with anyone so insignificant as the Cit to whom she had been introduced that night at Covent Garden.

"I am well aware that my life has changed, my lord, but how that can affect you, I cannot imagine."

"Can you not? And I had thought you awake upon every suit! I refer, of course, to freedom, my dear. As a married woman, you are allowed certain, shall we say, privileges, that unmarried ladies are denied. Should you decide to avail yourself of them, I would be most happy to assist you."

"I'm sure you would — right into divorce and scandal."

"Scandal?" echoed the earl. "'Tis done all the time, I assure you. I'll wager half the men of the *ton* are raising one another's bastards. In the case of your weaver, why, he should be grateful to me for doing my humble best to improve his bloodlines."

Lady Helen stiffened. "You are offensive, Waverly," she said frostily.

The earl's eyebrows rose. "I beg your pardon; I never realized Mr. Brundy had so ardent a champion. But if you fear to lose all that lovely money in a divorce, my dear, you may set your mind at ease. Your husband has, by whatever means, aligned himself with the family of a duke. I assure you, he will gladly turn a blind eye to his wife's indiscretions rather than lose the connection."

"How little you know him, if you believe that!" scoffed Lady Helen. "Mr. Brundy fancies himself the equal of any Radney ever born."

"Ah! Then this little jaunt to Almack's is meant to put the upstart in his place?"

There was no point in denying it. "I suppose so," she shrugged.

Lord Waverly chuckled. "'Tis a pity, for you are wasted on the weaver, my dear. You deserve a man who is your equal — in every way." His long slender fingers cupped her chin and tipped her face up toward his. "I could be that man, Helen."

Lady Helen had never questioned her ability to handle Lord Waverly — nor any other man, for that matter. But she was suddenly aware that his tall figure blocked the way to the heavy curtain which separated this chamber from the assembly room, and the discovery made her heart beat faster. Still, it would never do to let Lord Waverly know that he had disconcerted her. Raising her fan to her mouth, she delicately stifled a yawn.

"Do you know, Waverly, I've just now realized that I really don't like you very much?"

Lord Waverly opened his mouth to reply, but was interrupted by a sudden commotion from without. The violins scraped to a halt as the sounds of raised voices and scuffling feet filled the assembly room.

"What the devil is happening out there?" Waverly grumbled.

Lady Helen seized the opportunity to slip past him, and emerged from the alcove to find a crowd gathered around the assembly room doors. Gripped by a sudden premonition, she edged her way through the crush until she reached the source of the disturbance. There, just inside the entrance, the master of ceremonies and a liveried porter struggled to evict a new arrival. Said arrival being loth to depart, the porter sought recourse to fisticuffs in order to carry out his duty.

"I tell you, me wife is in 'ere!" insisted the intruder, resisting the porter's best efforts to eject him. "If you'll only listen for 'alf a minute —"

"Mr. Brundy!" shrieked Lady Helen, unwittingly distracting her husband just long enough to give the porter the opening he needed to land a solid blow to his adversary's jaw.

100

"'ullo, 'elen, me dear," Mr. Brundy said, then, smiling beatifically at his wife, crumpled to a heap at her feet.

"He has put himself completely beyond the pale," Lady Helen informed her father as she paced the Aubusson carpet in the duke's drawing room, her willow green skirts swirling about her with every turn. "One may, if one has sufficient funds, purchase a house in the best part of Mayfair. One may even, if one is well-connected enough, insult the membership of White's and live to tell the tale. But one may never, *ever,* set foot in Almack's Assembly Rooms without first being granted vouchers by one of the patronesses!"

"And 'ow was I supposed to know that?" asked Mr. Brundy, holding a raw beefsteak to his rapidly swelling jaw.

Lady Helen whirled about to confront the cause of her humiliation. "All the *ton* knows it!"

"I am not the *ton,*" declared Mr. Brundy, displaying a hitherto unsuspected talent for understatement.

"I could not have said it better myself!" retorted Lady Helen.

His Grace the Duke listened to their marital bickering with growing impatience. "Sit down, Helen, and stop flinging yourself about. Remember, you are still a Radney."

Obediently, Lady Helen took her place beside her husband on the settee, but when Mr. Brundy patted her hand consolingly, she snatched it away.

"That said, I am afraid my daughter is quite right," the duke informed his son-in-law. "You will certainly be *persona non grata* at Almack's, at least for the rest of the season."

Mr. Brundy had no knowledge of Latin, but he had not amassed a fortune by being stupid, and had no difficulty understanding that his presence there would not be welcomed.

"No great loss," he said, shrugging his shoulders in resignation. "I didn't like it above 'alf, anyway."

"Quite right," agreed the hitherto silent viscount, finding himself in perfect charity with his disgraced brother-in-law. "The tea is weak, the cakes are stale, and the —"

"Hold your tongue, Theodore!" growled the duke, and the chastened viscount lapsed once more into silence. Having dealt with his son and heir, the duke turned his attention back to his errant son-in-law. "As my daughter says, you have certainly put yourself beyond the pale. Still, you are a part of this family now, and I will use my influence to see that you get over the ground as lightly as you can. First of all, you must remind the *ton* of your close connection with the noble house of Radney."

"And 'ow am I to do that, sir?"

"Tell me, what think you of the name Ethan Radney?"

Mr. Brundy nodded his approval. "It 'as a fine

ring to it, it does. Per'aps the viscount might wish to give it to 'is son someday."

Viscount Tisdale, having already come to his brother-in-law's defense once, was understandably reluctant to incur his father's wrath by doing so again. He slumped down in his chair and tried very hard to become invisible.

"I am not speaking of my son, you nodcock!" snapped the duke. "I am giving you permission to assume one of the oldest, most honored names in England!"

"I'm afraid I'll 'ave to decline the honor, your Grace," replied Mr. Brundy.

"Decline? Poppycock! Why should you?"

"It took me twenty-three years to 'ave a name of me own. Now that I've got one, I'm in no 'urry to give it up."

The duke was not accustomed to having his will crossed, and the experience caught him off guard. "You are no doubt overcome by the honor being offered you," he growled. "I am certain you will see the wisdom of such a course, once you have had time to consider the matter."

Mr. Brundy was equally certain that no amount of consideration would change his mind, but as he had no desire to quarrel with his father-in-law, he wisely held his tongue.

"Next," continued the duke, "you must separate yourself from your unfortunate beginnings in Trade. You must sell your mill."

"Begging your pardon, your Grace, but I'll do no such thing."

Mr. Brundy never raised his voice, but the effect of his declaration was profound nonetheless. Both Radney siblings ceased breathing, watching their father warily and waiting for his wrath to descend. Neither Lady Helen nor her brother lacked spirit, but they had grown up from the cradle with the understanding that the duke's every whim was to be obeyed without question. The viscount's peccadilloes might have gotten him sent down from Oxford, but where his father was concerned, he was aware of a line which he dared not cross. Even Lady Helen, who prided herself on her independence of spirit, had gone meekly enough to the altar with the man of her father's choosing. As she watched her father's face turn crimson with rage, she could not but wonder if he was still happy with his choice.

"You, sir, will do as I say!" the duke barked. "You forget you are addressing the head of the house of Radney!"

Mr. Brundy shook his head. "Seeing as 'ow the 'ead of the 'ouse of Radney couldn't manage 'is own affairs without running himself to ground, I'll be 'anged if I'll let 'im tell me 'ow to manage mine."

The duke's coloring darkened from crimson to purple. "So you think to lord it over me with your money, do you?"

"Not at all. When you gave me permission to address your daughter, you told me not to think me money gave me the right to dictate to you. Might I suggest, your Grace, that what's sauce for the goose is sauce for the gander?"

For one tense moment the duke struggled with himself. Then his coloring gradually returned to normal, and he nodded. "Very well, Mr. Brundy," he said, with a gleam in his eye which suggested he was not entirely displeased to discover that his son-in-law possessed a backbone, although he would have cut out his tongue before admitting to such a thing.

While Lady Helen's flawless complexion did not change color, a transformation no less profound was taking place within. As she listened to her husband quietly but firmly stand up to the duke, the first seeds of respect for the man she had married began to take root. What was it about a misbegotten workhouse orphan that made no less a personage than the duke of Reddington back down before him?

"— you should still look the gentleman," the duke was saying as Lady Helen forced her attention back to the conversation in progress. "I have an appointment with my tailor on Friday morning. You will —" he hesitated, regarding his son-in-law with a sardonic gaze. "That is, I should be pleased if you would accompany me, Mr. Brundy."

"I should be 'appy to, your Grace, but I'm afraid I'll 'ave to pass. I've been away from the mill too long, and must return to Lancashire for a few days."

"You're going away?" asked Lady Helen, taken by surprise.

"I'd be pleased to show you the mill, if you'd like to accompany me," offered Mr. Brundy.

Lady Helen, already regretting her moment of weakness, gave a disdainful sniff. "I am already painfully aware that I owe my sustenance to Trade without being reminded of the fact, sir."

Mr. Brundy nodded his acquiescence. "In that case, me dear, I'll see you when I return."

"And when might that be?"

"Just as soon as the 'orses can get me 'ere," he replied, and the warmth in his brown eyes made Lady Helen's face grow heated.

"Take all the time you need, Mr. Brundy," she said with crushing civility.

7

Oh, how many torments lie
in the small circle of a wedding ring!
COLLEY CIBBER, *The Double Gallant*

Lady Helen remained abed until well past noon, recovering from the effects of her late night. When she at last made her appearance below, she saw no sign of her husband, either in the breakfast room or the drawing room. She dismissed his absence as a matter of little interest, supposing him to be either cloistered in his study or tending to business at his London warehouse.

When he did not appear for tea, she wondered if he might be visiting Brooks's or White's with his cronies — although it was a wonder to her that he should have the effrontery to show his face abroad, after the previous evening's fiasco at Almack's.

When she took her place at the dinner table and found it laid for one, however, Lady Helen was perplexed enough to question the butler as to her husband's whereabouts.

"Mr. Brundy departed for Manchester early

this morning," Evers informed her. "He left this for you, my lady, to be given to you, should you inquire."

Having delivered himself of this speech in a tone which, although scrupulously polite, clearly communicated his opinion that she should have inquired long before now, Evers presented her with a letter, folded and sealed with a wafer.

"Thank you, Evers," said Lady Helen, dismissing the butler with a nod.

After he had quit the room, she broke the seal and spread the single sheet. Concealed within its folds were five twenty-pound notes, along with the name and direction of her husband's banker. Should she find herself in need of additional funds, read this epistle, she had only to apply to this gentleman, as he had been instructed to advance her whatever amount she might require. Until his return he was, as ever, her most devoted Ethan B.

Lady Helen read the note a second time, then a third. He was gone. He had left that morning, without even saying goodbye.

Biting back a most unladylike whoop, Lady Helen hurried to her writing desk and dashed off a hasty missive to her father and brother, begging for the pleasure of their escort to Covent Garden later that evening. After dispatching a footman to deliver this communication, she flung herself into the task of deciding which one of her new gowns she would wear to the theater.

The duke and the viscount did not disappoint

her, and soon the trio was ensconced in the duke's box, from which location the *ton* was made privy to the information that Lady Helen had shed, at least for the nonce, her gauche bridegroom. The discovery brought her former suitors flocking to the ducal box during the intermission, and chief among their number was the ubiquitous earl of Waverly.

"Lady Helen," he said, bowing over her hand. "An unexpected pleasure, seeing you alone."

"But I am not alone, my lord," she protested with feigned misunderstanding. "My father and brother are with me."

"So they are," conceded the earl, eyeing the duke and viscount in a manner that would have cheerfully consigned them to the devil. "And yet, one of your coterie is absent, is he not? Where, pray, is the fascinating Mr. Brundy?"

"He is gone to Manchester."

"Ah, ever the conscientious tradesman, our Mr. Brundy. Or has he been exiled from Society for his sins?"

Lady Helen pinned Waverly with an unblinking gaze. "I do not discuss my husband with you, my lord."

"As you wish," replied the earl with an ironic lift of his eyebrow.

The signal for the beginning of the next act precluded further conversation, but Lady Helen could not in truth say she was sorry. Nor, for that matter, could she pay much attention to the scenes being enacted on the stage. While she agreed with her brother that the tragedy was indeed overlong but the farce which followed vastly diverting, she could not have stated with certainty what either of them was about. Her gaze kept straying across the pit to the boxes on the other side, and particularly to the one nearest the proscenium arch. It was from that vantage point that Mr. Brundy had watched her so disconcertingly on the night they were first introduced. To be sure, if she had known where that first introduction was to lead, she might have been tempted to fling herself over the parapet.

It was well past midnight by the time the duke's crested carriage deposited Lady Helen at her front door. Evers was waiting to throw open the door for her, and she passed through into the shadowy hall, where only a few candles burned. She thanked the butler and told him he might go to bed, then made her way across the hall to the stairs.

Her footsteps echoed on the marble tiles and the stairs stretched up into darkness, making the house which had been her home for the last two weeks seem eerie and unfamiliar. She picked up a branched candelabrum from a side table at the foot of the stairs and began her ascent, making a mental note to instruct Evers to keep the house fully lit the next time she went out.

Upstairs, she passed the door of her husband's bedchamber, where no light burned, and found herself wondering where he was at that moment, and what he was doing. Annoyed by the maudlin turn her thoughts had taken, she retired to her own chamber and, finding her abigail nodding at her post, dismissed the weary woman more sharply, perhaps, than was necessary.

While Lady Helen lingered before the door of his vacant bedchamber, Mr. Brundy lay slumbering at a posting house in Stafford, where he had broken his journey for the night. He resumed his travels early the next morning, having never completely broken his lifelong habit of rising with the sun. He reached his destination shortly after noon, and tarried only long enough to partake of a cold collation before presenting himself at his place of business.

The sprawling brick building, situated some twelve miles north of the city, was ugly by architectural standards, but Mr. Brundy's heart swelled with pride at the sight of it nonetheless. He dragged open the heavy door, then paused on the threshold while his eyes adjusted to the twilight world within.

"Ethan!" A familiar voice rose above the drone of the steam-powered machinery. "Ethan, me lad, where ye been? Ye've been away from us too long, ye have!"

Mr. Brundy followed the sound to an aging worker whose wide grin bore witness to the shortcomings of north country dentistry.

"Ben! 'ow in the world are you?" demanded

Mr. Brundy, clapping this individual heartily on the back in spite of the lint and perspiration that clung to him.

"Never mind me, lad! Stand back an' let me have a look at ye. My, but ye look fine as fivepence!" pronounced Ben, filled with admiration for the same blue morning coat and yellow pantaloons which had so pained the duke upon their first interview. "Still, exceptin' that yer dressed like a regular Lunnon toff, ye haven't changed a bit."

"Aye, that I 'ave, Ben," confessed Mr. Brundy with a grin. "You be'old me a married man!"

The older man's reaction was all that Mr. Brundy might have wished. "Married?" he exclaimed. "Never say so! When?"

"These two weeks and more. I'd 'oped to bring me wife to meet you, but —"

"Two weeks wed, an' ye've left yer bride to come here? Ye'll never get a son on her that way! Who's the lucky girl?"

"I don't know 'ow lucky she considers 'erself," said Mr. Brundy, electing to ignore the earthier parts of this speech, "but me wife is Lady 'elen Radney — leastways she was, until she married me."

"*Lady* — ?"

Mr. Brundy nodded. "Daughter of 'is Grace, the Dook of Reddington."

A long hiss of escaping steam seemed to echo Ben's sentiments.

"Ye hear that?" he bellowed to anyone within

hearing. "Our Ethan has gone an' married hisself a duchess!"

"Well, not a duchess, exactly," the bridegroom offered apologetically, but no one seemed to pay him any heed.

"What's she like, Mr. Brundy, sir?" asked one of the younger workers, a bashful lad of eighteen who had not Ben's advantage of long acquaintance with his employer, and who consequently regarded that legendary figure with an awe which bordered on idolatry. "Is she pretty?"

"As a rose in May," replied Mr. Brundy proudly.

"And sweeter nor any angel, I'll be bound," put in another.

Mr. Brundy chuckled and shook his head. "I'm afraid you're fair and far off there, John. A regular shrew she is, me lady wife."

"Then why'd you marry her?" retorted John, unconvinced.

"I'd no choice," Mr. Brundy said simply. "I took one look at 'er, and me 'eart was no longer me own."

"What I'd really like to know," said John, "is why *she* married *you!*"

"For 'is money, o' course!" a burly redhead chimed in.

The guffaws which greeted this sally were so boisterous that no one noticed Mr. Brundy's laughter was somewhat forced. He was spared the necessity of a reply by the appearance of a lean young man with straight fair hair, who hurried up the wide aisle which separated the rows of steam-powered spinners bearing a letter in one hand. The other hand, his left, was missing; the empty sleeve was rolled up and neatly pinned below the elbow.

"Mr. Brundy, sir!" called this new arrival as he bore down upon the group.

"What's toward, Tommy?" asked Mr. Brundy, grateful for the interruption.

"'Tis from Nottingham, sir," replied Tommy, producing the letter. "The roller printing machine you ordered won't be here till next week."

Since the main reason Mr. Brundy had torn himself away from his bride was to see to the installation of the aforementioned machine, he was perhaps understandably displeased with the news. Not being one to kill the messenger simply because he disliked the message, however, he resisted the urge to vent his frustration on his employee.

"Well, then, I suppose I'll 'ave to make other plans," he said, suppressing a sigh of exasperation at the prospect of another trip to Manchester and yet another week away from his wife. Resigning himself to the inevitable, he followed Tommy to the office and allowed himself to be brought up to date on the situation. No sooner had Tommy taken his leave than there was a knock on the office door, and a moment later Ben's grizzled head appeared in the opening.

"Ethan, I'd like a word wi' ye, if ye don't mind."

The younger man motioned the elder inside. "No, of course not, Ben. Come in."

Ben did so, and shut the door firmly behind him. "Lad, I'll not mince words. What's the matter wi' ye?"

The question, as well as the manner in which it was asked, caught Mr. Brundy off guard. "I beg your pardon?"

"Ye heard me, Ethan. I've knowed ye nigh on twenty years, an' I've watched ye grow up from a sprout. Somethin' happened when Jack started ribbin' ye about yer money — or was it your wife?" Mr. Brundy not being inclined to respond, Ben added, "Ye should know ye can't fool ol' Ben."

"Apparently not," said Mr. Brundy with a singularly humorless laugh. "If you must know, Jack 'it the nail on the 'ead. She wed me for me money, Ben."

Ben found this hard to believe. "A duke's daughter, marrying for money? Bah!"

"'appens all the time in 'igh Society, believe me. Seems the Dook 'as a weakness for cards. 'e wanted funds, and I wanted 'is daughter, so we struck a bargain. I guess you could say as 'ow I bought 'er for seventy-five thousand pounds."

"Seventy-five thousand pounds?" Ben echoed incredulously. "Gawd! Wish I had a couple o' girls I could sell ye!"

Mr. Brundy's lips twitched, but he offered no comment.

Ben pressed on. "An' ye love her, this duchess o' yers?"

"More than life."

"Well, ye married above yer station, lad, an' I'm thinkin' ye'll have to take what comes with it," replied the older man, albeit not without sympathy. "Still an' all, I can't say as I'm sorry you did. It'll be one in the eye for old Wilkins. He's been thinkin' to foist his gal Becky on you, even though she and Tommy are mad for each other."

This, it seemed, was news to his employer. "Tommy wants to marry Becky Wilkins?"

"Aye, has this last year an' more, but her pa wouldn't hear of it, not so long as there were a bigger fish to be caught."

"If Tommy's thinking to support a wife, 'e'll want a raise in wages," observed Mr. Brundy.

"I expect he wouldn't turn it down. Might bring Papa Wilkins around, too."

"Send him to me on your way out," instructed Mr. Brundy, giving Ben to understand that his private interview was at an end. The older man obeyed without protest, but paused at the door to offer one last word of advice.

"Yer a good man, Ethan, an' I couldn't be prouder of ye if ye were me own son. If that duchess o' yers is half the woman ye deserve, she'll be on her knees thankin' her Maker for her good fortune."

Mr. Brundy spent four days at his mill, addressing his workers' concerns and reacquainting himself with the business which, he feared, he had sadly neglected since his arrival in London. Nor was his wife idle during his absence. Lady Helen was everywhere to be seen, shopping in Bond Street or driving in St. James Park by day, and waltzing at Vauxhall Gardens or attending the opera by night. Certainly no one seeing her twirling about the dance floor or laughing at some admirer's flowery compliments would have suspected that this whirlwind of activity was Lady Helen's way of avoiding a house which had somehow become too large and too quiet, and where her heart had developed an annoying tendency to leap every time she heard a footfall in the hall below.

It was on one of these excursions to Vauxhall that Lord Waverly waylaid her as she admired the Grand Cascade.

"Ah, Mrs. Brundy," he drawled as he made his bow. "Is your husband not yet returned? So sad, seeing a bride neglected."

"Am I neglected, my lord?" asked Lady Helen in some surprise. "I did not know it."

"Forgive me; it would seem I am in error. Still," he added, lowering his voice to a conspiratorial whisper, "if ever you should find you are lonely, you have only to send for me, my dear."

"If I do that, Waverly, you may be sure that I must be very, very lonely indeed," Lady Helen replied, then turned and walked away.

She had not gone far before she was joined by

Lord David Markham and Sir Aubrey Tabor, both of whom had been present at her wedding.

"Good evening, Lady Helen," said Sir Aubrey, bowing over her hand. "I say, where have you been keeping that husband of yours? I haven't seen Ethan this age."

"He is in Manchester, attending to his mill."

Lord David's brow furrowed. "Not trouble with the Luddites, I hope?"

Lady Helen drew a complete blank. "Luddites?" she echoed. "What are they?"

"Bands of men who attack the mills and destroy the machinery," explained Sir Aubrey helpfully.

"They riot only at night, while the mills are unoccupied, and I do not believe it is their intention to harm persons," Lord David added hastily, seeing Lady Helen's eyes grow round. "I am not aware of any recent rioting in Manchester, and I am sure Ethan would have told you, had he believed himself to be in any danger."

"Of course," said Lady Helen, but privately she was not so sure.

She graciously accepted Lord David's invitation to join them in his supper box, where Emily, Lady Randall, was already ensconced, and allowed Sir Aubrey to procure for her a cup of rack punch and a plate of the paper-thin slices of ham for which Vauxhall was famous. But in spite of these amenities, she could not consider the evening an unqualified success. The music seemed too loud and the soprano too shrill, and although the others of the party seemed to have no complaints, even the celebrated ham tasted slightly off.

Upon her return home, she ordered Evers to snuff out the candles burning in the hall, then climbed the stairs to her bedchamber. She allowed her abigail to undress her and take down her hair, but even after dismissing the maid, she did not go immediately to bed. Instead she crossed the room to the small table that stood beside the bed, pulled open the single drawer, and removed a creased sheet of paper. She had kept the note without knowing precisely why; now she spread the folds and scanned the familiar lines. Should she find herself in need of additional funds . . . instructed to advance . . . whatever amount she might require . . . until his return he was, as ever, her most devoted Ethan B.

There was no clue as to precisely why he had gone or when he expected to return, only that he did plan to do so. That his journey might be a protracted one was suggested by his provisions for her to have additional funds as needed. Good heavens! Did the man not realize that she could have gone to his banker with some Banbury tale, then taken every farthing he owned and fled to the Continent?

Unless, perhaps, he had not thought to need money where he was going. Perhaps he had gone to his banker to put his affairs in order in case he did not come back. Perhaps she was even now a wealthy widow. Perhaps at this very moment a courier was en route from Manchester with the news. She glanced at the ormolu clock on the mantle, its ticking noise the only sound in the room. How long would it take for word of his death to reach her? She had resented the loss of her freedom, but now, faced with the possibility of regaining it, she no longer wanted to be free — at least, not at the cost of Mr. Brundy's life.

Nonsense, she chided herself. Lord David had said that the Luddites did not set out to injure people, but machines. Depend upon it, Mr. Brundy was alive and well in Manchester, and would no doubt be vastly amused to know that she had worried about him. Well, he would pay for frightening her so! *Oh, have you been gone?* she would say when he returned. *I hadn't noticed.* She crawled into bed and snuffed out the candle, but sleep did not come quickly.

She awoke in the chill gray hours before dawn to the sound of raindrops beating against the window. Thunder rumbled in the distance, and then again, much nearer. Lady Helen sat bolt upright. That last was not thunder, but the sound of carriage wheels rolling to a stop before the front door. Jerking back the bed curtains, she leaped out of bed, ran to the window, and pressed her face against the cold glass.

A post chaise was stopped in the street below, and as she watched, the door opened and a dark figure, hunched over to protect itself from the rain, scrambled down from the carriage and hurried up the front steps and out of Lady Helen's range of vision. A moment later she heard voices, and then the now-familiar ring of footsteps on the tiled floor of the hall. She fumbled with her candle in the dark until it finally flared to life, then shrugged on her dressing gown and peered out her door just as the footsteps reached the top of the stairs.

"Mr. Brundy?"

His every movement bespoke exhaustion, but he turned at the sound of her voice. He had shed his drenched greatcoat and hat, but wet tendrils of dark curly hair clung to his forehead, the drops of water trembling on the ends sparkling like diamonds in the candlelight.

"Ah, 'elen, you're a sight for sore eyes," he said with a contented sigh. "I've missed you, me dear."

Lady Helen chose to ignore this admission. "How are you, Mr. Brundy?" she asked, for all the world as if she were entertaining a morning caller.

"Fagged out, but other than that, well enough."

"You're sure? No trouble with the — the Luddites, or anything of that nature?"

A smile touched Mr. Brundy's lips. "Now, what do you know of the Luddites?"

This was too much for Lady Helen to bear. "Only that they might have killed you!" she retorted, goaded beyond endurance. "Which is more than *you*, sir, saw fit to tell me! 'Tis a fine thing when a woman must learn from her husband's friends that his life may be in danger! Well, I hope you enjoyed yourself, capering all over the country while I sat here frantic with worry! I bid you good night!"

Having delivered herself of this speech, she shut the door in his face. Mr. Brundy, far from being offended, lingered in the corridor, regarding his wife's closed door with a singularly foolish smile playing about his mouth. She had missed him. More than that, she actually cared whether he lived or died. Whistling softly under his breath, he disappeared into his own bedchamber and soon slept the sleep of the just.

Lady Helen arose before her husband the next morning, a reversal of their usual routine which was hardly surprising, given the length of his journey and the lateness of his arrival. Although the rain still pelted passers-by in the street and kept morning callers away, all was oddly at peace within the Brundy household. The house itself, which had only yesterday seemed so large and empty, had miraculously resumed its usual proportions during the night, and Lady Helen was no longer aware of the sound of her echoing footsteps as she crossed the hall.

Curiously enough, for the first time in a week she felt no need to fill her morning hours with frenzied activity. In fact, she was contentedly reading in the drawing room when her husband emerged from hibernation, shaved and dressed with his usual disregard for taste.

"Good morning, 'elen," he said cheerfully.

"Good morning, Mr. Brundy," she replied, although the hour was in fact past two o'clock.

"I'm off to 'ave a bit of breakfast, and then I've a few loose ends to tie up. I'll be in me study, if you should 'ave need of me."

"Very well." She watched as he turned to leave the room, whistling under his breath. As he reached the door, she called him back, her voice stiff as if the words were somehow forced from her unwilling throat. "Oh, and Mr. Brundy —"

He paused in the doorway to turn back. "Yes, me dear?"

"Welcome home."

Mr. Brundy smiled uncertainly at his bride. "I'm afraid it won't be for long. I've a new roller printing machine arriving from Nottingham next week, and I'll need to be on 'and to see it installed. You'll be rid of me for a while longer."

"Oh."

Once more he began to leave the room, and once more she called him back.

"Mr. Brundy?"

"Yes?"

"If you've no objection, I — I would be pleased to accompany you." Mr. Brundy's expressive countenance registered first surprise, then pleasure. "Nothing would make me 'appier."

8

Marriage has many pains,
but celibacy has no pleasures.
SAMUEL JOHNSON, *Rasselas*

While his wife made preparations for the journey to Lancashire, Mr. Brundy, under the auspices of his ducal papa-in-law, submitted himself to the tender mercies of Schweitzer and Davidson, tailors to no less a personage than the Prince Regent himself. The duke, having recently settled his delinquent account thanks in large part to Mr. Brundy's lavish marriage settlement, was welcomed to the venerable Cork Street establishment with open arms. His son-in-law's reception, however, was considerably cooler. The two tailors bobbed and bowed before his Grace, leaving their underling, Jennings, with the task of giving the boot to the badly dressed Cit who entered the shop in the duke's wake.

"Good morning, your Grace, and how may we be of service to you, your Grace? Not you, sir," said Jennings, gently but firmly closing the door in Mr. Brundy's face. "We don't do business with the likes of you. May I suggest you try Nugee? I understand he is less discriminating. So sorry, your Grace."

"So you should be, for you have just shut the door on my son-in-law!" barked the affronted duke.

Instantly Mr. Brundy found the door thrown wide to receive him. "Come in, come in, sir, I beg your pardon, Mr., er —"

"Brundy," he said, offering his hand. "Ethan Brundy."

"Mr. Brundy, sir," mumbled the hireling, uncomfortably accepting the handshake of one who, as his social superior, should have been above overtures which could only be described as familiar.

Mr. Schweitzer, the senior partner, listened in silence to this exchange. As his livelihood depended upon the fortunes of the *haut ton,* he made it his business to follow the latest *on dits,* whether published in the London papers or let fall from the lips of his noble clientele. He knew that all of London was abuzz with the news of the duke's daughter's hasty marriage to a wealthy tradesman, and this information, combined with the recent settlement of his Grace's long-overdue account, gave him a very fair idea of Mr. Brundy's importance to himself and his partner.

"And how may we be of service to you, Mr. Brundy?" he asked, almost tripping over his own feet in his haste to relieve the weaver of his hat and gloves.

125

"My son-in-law is recently arrived from Lancashire," the duke informed them. "He wishes you to turn him out as a gentleman."

"Indeed," said Mr. Schweitzer, eyeing his new client dubiously. "If you would remove your, er, coat, Mr. Brundy?"

Mr. Brundy obliged. "Where should I put it?" he asked.

"You might try the fireplace," suggested Jennings *sotto voce,* taking the offending garment between thumb and forefinger.

Ordering their underling to fetch a measuring tape, the royal tailors laid violent hands on the unfortunate Mr. Brundy and soon stripped him to his smallclothes, whereupon they stepped back to survey the canvas upon which they were to produce their art.

"Not above the average height, more's the pity, but the legs are well shaped, and the shoulders are broad," pronounced Mr. Schweitzer at last.

Nodding his agreement, Mr. Davidson, the junior partner, produced an assortment of fashion plates featuring pen-and-ink renderings of absurdly wasp-waisted gentlemen in tailcoats and breeches. "And for the proper silhouette, we might nip in the waist with a Cumberland corset —"

"I'll 'ang first!" declared an indignant Mr. Brundy, feeling very much like a horse on the block at Tattersall's.

"I think we can dispense with the corset," agreed Mr. Schweitzer, who knew which side his bread was buttered on. "While Mr. Brundy's waist is not as narrow as one might wish, at least he has no paunch. I think we can do something with him, your Grace."

Satisfied on this head, they set upon their hapless client with a measuring tape, Jennings duly writing down each measurement while Mr. Davidson clucked mournfully over the wonders a Cumberland corset might have wrought. Their task complete, they surrendered the prisoner's clothing and set him free, bowing their new client from the premises with all the reverence due an order totaling almost £200. Having seen both duke and commoner on their way, the royal tailors turned their attention to their errant employee.

"Oh, Jennings," said Mr. Schweitzer, "about your recommendation that Mr. Brundy place his coat on the fire —"

"I beg your pardon, sir," stammered the humbled Jennings. "I meant no offense. 'Twas only that —"

The senior tailor shook his head. "Wool burns far too slowly to suit the purpose, and it smells abominably."

Mr. Brundy and his bride departed for Manchester five days later, traveling at a more leisurely pace than he had set while traveling alone. Consequently, night had fallen by the time they broke their journey at Warwick. Mr. Brundy bespoke a private parlour at the Rose and

Crown, and they sat down to a simple but satisfying repast of boiled chicken and vegetables before climbing the narrow staircase to their room.

Here Lady Helen froze on the threshold. The room was tidy but small, its furnishings limited to a bed, a single straight chair, a wash stand on which stood a bowl and pitcher, and a rag rug before the fireplace in which a cheery fire burned.

Mr. Brundy, climbing the stairs in his wife's wake, surveyed the room over her shoulder and formed a fair estimation of her thoughts. "You can 'ave the bed, 'elen. I'll sleep on the rug."

Lady Helen examined first the rug, then her husband. He was not a tall man, but even the most cursory glance revealed that his feet — or his head, whichever he preferred — would certainly extend onto the bare floor.

"Nonsense," she said with a bravado which she was far from feeling. "We are, after all, man and wife, and there is no reason why we should not share the bed — provided we each stay on our own side," she added as a caveat, lest he should think to take advantage of a situation which neither of them had anticipated.

As Mr. Brundy had no real desire to make his bed on the floor, he conceded to this plan, and the pair turned their attentions to the portmanteaux which had been deposited beside the bed by the innkeeper's strapping son. Here, too, problems arose, as Lady Helen looked in vain for a private spot where she might change into her nightrail. Once again, Mr. Brundy rose to the occasion.

"I think I'll 'ave a look about the tap-room before I retire," he said, and promptly suited the word to the deed.

Alone in the tiny room, Lady Helen removed her travel-stained carriage dress and quickly donned her nightclothes, uncertain how long she might count on her husband to remain below. When this task had been completed with no sign of him, she took down her hair and brushed it out, and by the time he returned, she had laid claim to one side of the bed and lay there with the counterpane drawn up to her chin.

Whether for the sake of his own modesty or the benefit of his wife's, Mr. Brundy snuffed out the candle before donning his nightshirt. But although Lady Helen could not see the man in bed beside her, she was fully conscious of his presence, and was reminded anew every time the mattress shifted beneath his weight.

As for Mr. Brundy, he was painfully aware that his lawfully wedded wife, whom he adored and whom he had promised not to touch for six months, lay mere inches away. Consequently, both man and wife lay ramrod-straight on either side of the bed, separated by as wide an expanse of clean white linen as they could contrive. Each too conscious of the other's presence to sleep, they lay for half an hour in complete silence before Lady Helen was emboldened to put it to the test.

"Mr. Brundy," she whispered. "Are you asleep?"

"Yes," whimpered her husband.

"Oh." Lady Helen pondered this reply, but knew not what to make of it. "Good night, Mr. Brundy."

"Good night, 'elen."

Eventually, however, the long journey took its toll, and the deep, regular breathing emitting from the other side of the bed informed Lady Helen that her husband was indeed asleep. For the first time since she had been ushered into the tiny chamber, she was able to relax, and soon her eyes grew quite heavy. As sleep overtook her, so too did the vague awareness that there was something strangely comforting about the rhythmic rise and fall of her husband's breathing. She rolled over, instinctively drawn to the sound.

Unfortunately, the slumbering Mr. Brundy also chose that moment to roll over — and as a result they met in the middle of the bed. Awake in an instant, Lady Helen scrambled for the safety of her own side, clutching the counterpane tightly to her palpitating heart. Without a word, Mr. Brundy picked up his pillow and headed for the hearth rug. This time his wife did not attempt to dissuade him.

At length Lady Helen fell into a disturbed sleep, only to awaken some time later to discover that the fire had burned itself out and the room held a distinct chill. The moon had risen, casting a pale silvery light onto the sleeping figure of her husband, huddled on the floor before the cold hearth. Something about the sight tugged at Lady Helen's heart. Dragging the counterpane from the mattress, she spread it over his recumbent form and slipped back into the bed.

Mr. Brundy awoke stiff and sore the next morning to find himself covered with the counterpane. After allowing himself the indulgence of a moment to marvel at his slumbering bride, he pulled on his breeches and donned a clean shirt, then went downstairs to order coffee and await his wife.

She joined him half an hour later, looking as fresh and well-rested as if she had never left London. Clearly, Lady Helen had not been troubled by the same sort of dreams which had made his own slumber a torment from which he wished never to awaken. By tacit agreement, neither mentioned the events of the previous evening, but the silence which reigned in the private parlor where they partook of breakfast told its own tale.

Tensions eased somewhat once they were on the road, where they achieved a companionable, if somewhat cautious, camaraderie. As her father's ducal seat was located in Devon, Lady Helen had rarely had occasion to visit the North, and she took as much pleasure in observing the changing scenery as her husband did in pointing it out to her. In this manner they reached Stafford, where they broke their journey for a second night. This time, however, Mr. Brundy was prepared. As the proprietor's buxom wife showed Lady Helen to the private parlor, Mr. Brundy arranged for their lodgings with her husband.

"*Two* rooms, you say?" said the skeptical innkeeper, his eyes narrowing in suspicion as Mr. Brundy slid an extra coin across the counter. "I run a respectable establishment here. I thought you said you was man and wife."

"And so we are, these three weeks and more." Seeing mine host was not convinced, he darted a quick glance toward the private parlor, assuring himself that Lady Helen was well out of earshot. "'Tis me wife," he confided in an undervoice. "She snores."

The innkeeper looked past his boarder to the beautiful woman standing before the fire. She had removed her bonnet, and her honey-colored hair glowed in the firelight. He shrugged. "I'd have thought it worth the inconvenience, myself, but it's your money."

Mr. Brundy thanked his host, then joined his wife in the private parlor. "'Tis all settled, 'elen," he informed her. "Tonight you'll 'ave a room of your own."

"Thank you, Mr. Brundy," Lady Helen said, giving him a shy smile.

"Think nothing of it, me dear," he said modestly.

After a far more restful night's sleep than either had enjoyed the previous evening, they resumed their journey the next morning, and reached their destination as the sun sank in the west. As the post chaise rolled to a stop, Mr. Brundy disembarked before a squarish brick house of no particular architectural distinction.

"'Tis not a fine 'ouse by London standards," he offered apologetically as he handed his wife down, "but I thought it grand enough when I in-'erited it."

"Then this house belonged to the first Mr. Brundy?" Lady Helen asked. "The one who left you the mill?"

"That it did. I've thought of selling it, but it suits me purposes. Not too close to the mill, but not too far away, and better than putting up at an inn any day. Still, if you've a fancy for something larger, I'll 'ave me man of business make inquiries."

"Pray do not sell your house on my account, Mr. Brundy, for I am hardly qualified to judge," protested Lady Helen. "After all, this is the first time I've seen it."

"But not the last, I 'ope," added her husband.

This won him a tentative smile from his bride and, much encouraged, he took her arm and led her up the path to the front door. Once inside, he introduced her to Mr. and Mrs. Gatewood, the couple who looked after the house in his absence and served as butler/gardener and house-keeper/cook, respectively, while he was in residence. They both made much over their employer's lovely and well-born bride, then tactfully took themselves off, Gatewood to bring in the couple's bags and his wife to prepare their evening meal.

This was served an hour later, by which time both Brundys had had ample opportunity to rest after their lengthy journey. They sat down to eat in the dining room, and although neither the room nor the table were nearly so grand as those in the Grosvenor Square house, Lady Helen could not feel this to be a disadvantage. It was, she discovered, rather cozy to be able to converse without shouting down the length of the dining table, and her husband's face, now that it was no longer hidden by the massive epergne in the center of the table, was surprisingly pleasant to look upon.

This last observation came as quite a shock, and Lady Helen was obliged to focus all her attention on her plate until such time as she could consider the implications of her discovery more closely.

"The meat is very good," she remarked midway through the meal, more in an effort to give her thoughts a safer direction than to compliment Mrs. Gatewood's culinary skills.

"Aye, I've always been partial to Mrs. Gatewood's way with roast beef," agreed Mr. Brundy. "Ever since I first tasted it at Mr. Brundy's table."

"I shall ask her for the receipt, if you like," offered Lady Helen.

"I would," said her husband. "And while you're about it, you might ask the Dook's cook about that salmon we 'ad the night I came to dinner."

"You liked it?" Lady Helen asked in some surprise. "You never said so."

"I was afraid you might 'ave the footman snatch me plate away if I let on," confessed Mr. Brundy with a twinkle in his eye.

Lady Helen shot him a darkling glance, but refused to take the bait. "And so you like roast beef and salmon with shrimp sauce. Do you know, Mr. Brundy, we have been wed for over three weeks, and I am only just beginning to realize how little I know about you?"

"Like what?"

"Oh, I don't know," Lady Helen said with a shrug. "Everything. What, for instance, is your favorite color?"

Mr. Brundy pondered this question as intently as if the fate of the Empire hung on his answer. "I'll 'ave to say green," he pronounced at last. "At one time I would've said blue, but that was before I saw you in that green thing you wore to Almack's."

"Nonsense, Mr. Brundy," said Lady Helen, annoyed to feel her face grow warm.

"And now," he said, ignoring this interruption, "'Tis you 'oo must answer."

"Very well. What do you wish to know?"

"'ow old are you, 'elen?"

"Why, Mr. Brundy, what an unhandsome thing to ask!" scolded Lady Helen. "I shall expect you to be very shocked to learn that I am turned one-and-twenty last March."

"That I am, but not for the reason you think. What were those London toffs thinking, letting you go so long without being wed?"

"Ah, so now you know the truth: you saved me from spinsterhood, Mr. Brundy. According to Papa, my shrewish disposition drove away all my suitors."

"Aye, I've a thick skin," said Mr. Brundy with a grin.

"You shall need it, for now it is my turn to ask, and I shall require you to answer your own question."

"I am eight-and-twenty," he replied.

"So you told us, on the night you came to dinner," she reminded him. "But that is not what I meant. Surely there must have been many women in Manchester who would have been happy to marry you. Why did you have to come to London for a wife?"

"Because that's where you were," he said simply.

Since he could not have known of her existence prior to his arrival in London, Lady Helen would have challenged the logic of this response, had she not been struck mute by the sudden realization that her husband was flirting with her. Over the course of her four London seasons, she had been the recipient of all manner of fulsome compliments, most of which she turned aside with varying degrees of impatience, if not outright scorn. Mr. Brundy's remarks, however, were far more disconcerting, and not easily dismissed. Almost she wished the epergne were there for her to hide behind. In its absence, she pushed back her chair and rose from the table.

"If you are going to talk flummery to me, Mr. Brundy, I shall leave you to your port."

To her surprise, he rose with her. "I've never been fond of drinking alone, 'elen. If you've finished your dinner, will you join me in a game of piquet before we retire?"

"Cards, Mr. Brundy? I am surprised to learn you play. I was under the impression that you didn't gamble."

"On the contrary. Lord David, Sir Aubrey, and I've been known to lose vast empires to one another, all in the space of an evening."

"Oh, make-believe!" she scoffed. "It is not at all the same thing."

"If you lack the imagination for it, me dear, there are other things we might wager."

Lady Helen arched a skeptical eyebrow. "Such as?"

"Kisses, for one."

Lady Helen's face flamed. "Mr. Brundy! Are you suggesting that I kiss you?" she demanded, unsure whether to be offended or amused.

He regarded her with a singularly sweet smile. "Only if you lose."

"You forget, sir, that the Radneys are gamesters at heart," retorted Lady Helen with a kindling eye. "I accept your wager."

While she went in search of writing materials

for tallying points, Mr. Brundy set up a card table before the drawing room fire. The unnecessary cards were removed from the pack and the remainder shuffled and dealt, and then the battle was joined in earnest.

Lady Helen was a tolerable card player, having learned many years previously that her father and brother made no allowance for feminine foibles, and she gained an early lead. However, a poor second hand and a worse third soon eroded her advantage, and by the time the fourth hand was dealt, she was growing increasingly nervous. Too late, she remembered that, while the Radneys were indeed notoriously fond of gaming, they had never been known for their luck.

Her agitation did not go unremarked by Mr. Brundy, who watched with a creased brow as the two of hearts slipped from his wife's trembling fingers and landed face up on the table.

"Oh, dear," she fretted, snatching up the card only to drop two more.

"It's been a long day," he remarked sympathetically. "Are you ready to call it a night, me dear?"

Up came Lady Helen's chin. "I always finish what I start, Mr. Brundy."

He acceded with a nod. "As you wish."

The fourth hand did not go well for Lady Helen, and Mr. Brundy had the edge going into the fifth. By the time the sixth and final hand was dealt, he had built up a commanding lead, but unfortunately for the sake of his courtship, his play began, unaccountably, to slip. Whether through carelessness or premature anticipation of his reward, he made several crucial errors in judgment, and twice forgot to record points to which he was entitled. As a result, when the points were tallied at last, Lady Helen emerged victorious.

"Well, Mr. Brundy, it appears you will not get your kiss after all," she said in a voice made smug by triumph.

"Indeed, it does," her husband agreed mournfully. "Still and all, you can't blame a man for trying. Per'aps tomorrow I'll 'ave better luck."

Lady Helen threw up a hand in protest. "No, no! I shall wager no more on kisses, Mr. Brundy."

"Frightened you, did I?" he asked, grinning broadly at her.

"Not at all," she replied with a show of her former hauteur. "'Twas a foolish wager to begin with, and you, sir, were no gentleman to propose it!"

"Per'aps not, but then, I am not a gentleman," he reminded her without apology. "There are times when that can be a great advantage."

Lady Helen smiled at him uncertainly, but could think of no suitable reply. Still, he regarded her steadily with a curious little half-smile playing about his mouth, and she found herself wondering what might have happened if she had lost. . . .

This line of thought was perhaps fortunately

interrupted by the sound of the mantle clock striking midnight.

"Good heavens, look at the time!" cried Lady Helen, leaping up in such haste that she almost tipped over the card table. "If I am to see this mill of yours in the morning, I had best seek my bed."

"Unkissed, as agreed," promised her husband, albeit not without regret.

"Just so, Mr. Brundy," she replied.

But she climbed the stairs feeling strangely as if she were the loser.

9

All work, even cotton spinning, is noble.
THOMAS CARLYLE, *Past and Present*

As the sun rose over the Pennines, the textile mills of the greater Manchester area came slowly to life. By ten o'clock in the morning, some ninety-nine mills operated at full capacity, with the notable exception of one brick structure situated twelve miles outside the city, where work had been temporarily suspended. This particular mill was witnessing a momentous event, for the door had been flung open to admit its beaming owner, bearing on his arm the most striking woman the workers had ever seen. The pair were almost of a height, but where he was dark, she was fair, and where he was solidly built, she was slender as a reed, and carried herself like a queen. Furthermore, her fashionable peach-colored walking gown and wide-brimmed gypsy hat had clearly not come from any of the local shops. Mr. Brundy, it seemed, had brought his "duchess" for their inspection.

And inspect her they did, with bulging eyes and gaping mouths, until Mr. Brundy was obliged to tell his bride, "They're not 'alf as dumb as they look."

Like monarchs on progress, they slowly made their way down the center aisle separating the rows of spinners on either side, Mr. Brundy pausing now and then to address one or another of his workers.

The workers, Lady Helen soon discovered, fell into one of two camps. The older men called him Ethan or, as in the case of Ben, "lad," and treated him much the same as they might a precocious nephew or grandson; the younger addressed him as "Mr. Brundy, *sir*," and regarded him with the sort of reverence due one who fell only a step short of deity. A notable exception, however, was soon discovered in the form of a small boy sweeping lint in the nether reaches of the cavernous room. As if to defy classification, the child dropped his broom with a shriek and ran to meet the newcomers.

"Mr. Brundy! Mr. Brundy!" the boy's high-pitched squeals rose over the noise of the machinery. "Did you bring me something from Lunnon-town?"

Mr. Brundy's brow puckered. "Was I supposed to do that?"

"You promised!" the child insisted, dancing with impatience.

"Well, now, let's see." Mr. Brundy squatted down to the boy's level and reached into the inside breast pocket of his coat, pretending to tug at something concealed therein. "I think I feel something."

The boy needed no further invitation. He set upon his employer with enthusiasm, all but ripping the coat from Mr. Brundy's back in his eagerness to claim the prize.

Not, reflected Lady Helen, that the loss would have been great even had the coat not survived the assault. Still, it was a very odd thing, but Mr. Brundy's ill-fitting garments no longer bothered her as much as they once had done. Was she growing accustomed to him, she wondered, or did such things simply not matter so much outside the Metropolis?

By this time the child had captured the promised treat, a peppermint stick wrapped in wax-coated paper. His eyes round with wonder, the boy thanked his benefactor as fervently as if he had just been presented with the crown jewels. Without warning, the memory of her wedding night bobbed to the surface of Lady Helen's mind, and once again she saw Mr. Brundy, resplendent in a dressing gown of polished chintz. *I'd like to 'ave young 'uns of me own, 'elen. . . .* Yes, Mr. Brundy would make an excellent father, although he would no doubt spoil his children beyond all bearing — experiencing vicariously, perhaps, the carefree childhood he had been denied. This thought raised another puzzling question, which she addressed to her husband as soon as the boy had returned to his broom.

"I am surprised that you would hire a child, Mr. Brundy," she remarked. "I was under the impression that you had strong views on the subject."

"Aye, that I do, and it went sorely against the grain with me," the weaver confessed. "But the lad's father was crippled in me employ, and now the boy is the family's only means of support."

"Can you not simply make his father an allowance?" Lady Helen suggested.

Mr. Brundy shook his head. "These are proud people, 'elen. They won't accept charity, even from one of their own. I'd no choice but to give the boy a job, although I won't let 'im work more than four hours a day, and I'll not 'ave 'im standing idle at a machine all day. At least pushing a broom gives him the freedom to move about a bit. 'Tis unnatural for young 'uns to be cooped up for long periods of time."

"Like you were," added Lady Helen sympathetically.

"Aye, like I was." Mr. Brundy shook his head, as if banishing old ghosts, and when he spoke again it was in a much lighter tone. "I should be pleased to show you the manufacturing process from start to finish, if you like."

Lady Helen smiled at her husband. "I should like that very much."

"This is the spinning room, and the machines you see are called spinning mules. The mules twist the cotton fibers into threads, and the threads feed the looms, which weave it into cloth. Now, right over 'ere —"

They proceeded to the power looms, where Lady Helen watched in fascination as thread turned to cloth before her eyes, while Mr. Brundy explained the three-step process of shedding, picking, and beating in. He was interrupted in this endeavor by the arrival of the one-armed Tommy.

"Mr. Brundy, sir —" he began, then checked at the sight of the lady accompanying his employer. "Oh, I beg your pardon!"

"'elen, this is Tommy. Tommy, meet me wife, Lady 'elen Brundy. You might say Tommy is me right 'and," he added as an aside to Lady Helen.

"Aye, for I can hardly be his left," replied Tommy with a grin, indicating his empty sleeve. "Sorry to interrupt, Mr. Brundy, but we've run into some trouble with the printing machine."

"I'll be right there," promised Mr. Brundy. "If you'll excuse me, 'elen? Tommy, would you show me wife about the place until I get back?"

Tommy grinned. "Glad to, Mr. B. Right this way, Mrs. Brundy."

Lady Helen allowed the misuse of her title to pass. The appellation, so galling on Lord Waverly's mocking lips, carried a very different connotation when Tommy spoke it.

"He certainly seems to know his business," she remarked, watching her husband's retreating back.

"Aye, none better," agreed Tommy. "Now, where did you get to?"

"Mr. Brundy was telling me how the looms work."

"Well, I should be able to do that, seeing as how I ran one for seven years," Tommy said proudly.

"Why did you stop?" asked Lady Helen.

"It's a two-handed job."

"Is that how you were injured?"

"Aye, four years ago come August. Mr. Brundy had just taken over the mill, and he felt partly to blame, even though it wasn't his fault. Still, he trained me as a sort of manager. I've had offers from some of the other mills, but I'll not work for anybody else. He really is the best of men." He paused, grinning sheepishly as he remembered his audience. "But you're his wife, so I guess you already know that."

Lady Helen smiled. "I'm beginning to."

"Lord, I'd give a monkey to have seen him in London amongst all the nobs! Cut a regular dash, I'll bet."

You were the laughingstock of London long before you married me. . . . The memory of her own words echoed in Lady Helen's head. No, she could not bring herself to shame him before these people who thought so highly of him. "He was — certainly eye-catching," she managed at last.

Encouraged by this revelation, Tommy continued to ply her with questions to which she was hard pressed to form answers without resorting to outright fabrication. In this manner, they reached a curious-looking apparatus dominated by a large cast-iron cylinder and several smaller rollers. A trio of sweating men struggled to coax the rollers to turn, while a fourth, laboring underneath the machine, was invisible save for his booted feet protruding out from under it.

"This," Tommy explained with a flourish, "is the new roller printing machine. Up to now, the woven cloth has been sent to Vint and Gilling for printing, but Mr. Brundy thought as how it could be done more cheaply under one roof."

Lady Helen took a closer look at the strange contraption, and thought she recognized the boots. In spite of their sadly scuffed condition, they were far more costly than those a mill worker might afford.

"Mr. Brundy?" she addressed the footwear. "Is that you?"

The boots stirred and then began to emerge, growing first legs and then a torso, until at last her husband's head appeared.

"'elen, me dear," he said, clambering to his feet. "I 'ope Tommy 'asn't been boring you."

Lady Helen, staring at her husband with new eyes, did not respond. His hair was mussed and a smudge of black grease stained his cheek. He had shed his coat and waistcoat, and the oppressive heat generated by the steam-powered machinery, combined with the exertion of physical labor, had plastered his thin cambric shirt to his body. The end result, while disheveled, held a certain raffish appeal. Lady Helen suppressed a strong urge to reach out and wipe the black smudge from his cheek.

"Boring me? Not at all," she said hastily.

"Mrs. Brundy has been telling me about the splash you made in London," put in Tommy.

Mr. Brundy regarded his wife warily. "'as she, now?"

"Lord, I wish I'd been there to see it!" Tommy enthused. "We're all proud of you, Mr. B."

He continued in this vein for some time, until his employer conveniently recalled a task that required Tommy's immediate attention, whereupon the conscientious worker hastily took his leave.

"Your workers are very loyal," remarked Lady Helen as she watched him make his way through rows of hissing and groaning machinery.

"It would seem they're not the only ones," replied Mr. Brundy, regarding his wife with a puzzled expression.

They left the mill a short time later, Mr. Brundy having taken a moment to remove his dirt before escorting his bride back home. Unfortunately, Tommy had by this time spread the word that Mr. Brundy's lady wife was not at all high in the instep — an observation which would have shocked her London acquaintances, had they been privy to it. Thus informed, the workers elected to notify their employer of their approval of his choice.

Consequently, as Mr. Brundy ushered his bride past row upon row of humming spinners, a shout rang out.

"Give 'er a kiss for us, boy!"

The cry was quickly taken up, and even some of the youthful worshippers were emboldened to join in. Seeing no other way to quiet the mob, Mr. Brundy gave his wife an apologetic look, followed by a chaste peck on the cheek.

This action found no favor with his workers, who greeted it with jeers and catcalls. In the end it was Jack (he whose laughing observations on his employer's marriage had so cut up Mr. Brundy's peace) who voiced the displeasure of the masses by demanding, "Didn't we learn you any better nor that?"

Turning toward her husband, Lady Helen was surprised to see the unflappable Mr. Brundy turn beet-red with embarrassment. Forgetting her own discomfiture, she raised her face ever so slightly to his.

"Yes, Mr. Brundy, surely you can do better than that," she murmured.

He gazed down at her with a question in his brown eyes. Finding the answer he sought in her green ones, he slowly bent and pressed a lingering kiss onto her expectantly parted lips, to the loud approval of the masses.

It was a silent and self-conscious pair who made their way outside. Mr. Brundy handed his wife into the gig, then climbed up after her and took the reins. Neither spoke for a full five minutes.

At last Mr. Brundy could bear it no longer. "All right, 'elen, let's 'ave it. What did you tell that boy to make 'im think I've got all of London at me feet?"

"I didn't tell him anything that wasn't true," insisted Lady Helen, instantly on the defensive. "I told him that you were on intimate terms with members of Parliament, and that you visit the gentlemen's clubs with peers of the realm, and that you —"

Here she faltered in her recital of his triumphs, and he was obliged to prompt her. "And that I what?"

"And that you took Almack's by storm," she confessed guiltily.

Mr. Brundy's lips twitched, and then he laughed aloud. "Aye, I did at that, didn't I?" He caught her hand and pressed it to his lips. "You're a brick, 'elen Brundy."

Lady Helen could not have said why this simple tribute warmed her heart so, but it did.

"Anyway, that's the mill," he said. "What did you think of it?"

Although his tone was nonchalant, there was something in his expression which betrayed his eagerness for her approbation. She found his imperfectly concealed anxiety rather sweet.

"I thought it was fascinating," she replied, and had the satisfaction of seeing the anxiety in his eyes replaced by pride.

And it *was* fascinating, she reflected, though not necessarily for the reasons he thought. Any one of Manchester's dozens of cotton mills could produce calico and gingham, but this one had produced a man. He had been tempered in the fires of poverty and hard labor, forged into a man unlike any Town beau she had ever known. He was the gentlest of men, yet he had held his ground against the Duke of Reddington's towering rage. He was an astute businessman, yet he treated his workers with consideration and fairness. He debated labor reform with members of Parliament, yet he took the trouble to buy peppermints for a child in his employ. In their three weeks of marriage, he had never responded in kind to her verbal barbs, but had shown her more kindness, perhaps, than she deserved.

The great irony was that there was no place in Society for such a man. However vast his fortune might be, it had been acquired through Trade, and that fact negated all other considerations. It might not be fair, but since when had life ever dealt fairly with workhouse orphans?

He should not have tried to fight it, she thought as the square brick house appeared over the hill. He should have stayed here, where he belonged, and married a girl of his own class who would have filled his house to the rafters with strapping boys and apple-cheeked girls.

The image, merry as it was, left her feeling strangely hollow inside.

10

Of all the icy blasts that blow on love,
a request for money is the most chilling.
GUSTAVE FLAUBERT, *Madame Bovary*

During Lady Helen's absence from London,
Lord Waverly consoled himself by furthering his
acquaintance with her young brother, Viscount
Tisdale. Since the earl was not in the habit of
lending consequence to green youths, the viscount could not but feel flattered when a
chance meeting at Tattersall's resulted in an invitation to accompany the earl to a new and already notorious gaming hell where, it was reputed, Lord Farley had won the astonishing
sum of £30,000 in a single night. That some
other, less fortunate soul must have lost an
equal sum on the same night did not in the least
deter the viscount's eagerness to try his own
luck. And so, armed with a rouleau of guineas
and an optimistic frame of mind, he set out for
Jermyn Street with his host.

Upon their arrival, young Tisdale was hard
pressed to hide his disappointment. The gaming

hell, viewed from the street, looked not at all like a den of iniquity, but a rather staid residence.

"This is it?" he asked his mentor in disbelief.

"Indeed, it is," confessed the earl. "I trust you will not be disappointed."

Waverly lifted the door knocker and let it fall. A pair of steely eyes inspected the newcomers through a slit in the door, and a moment later they were admitted by a burly porter whose crooked nose suggested a prior career as a pugilist. Once inside, the viscount found the atmosphere far more in keeping with his expectations. A cloud of cigar smoke hung in the air, and the scent of strong spirits stung his nostrils. Tisdale followed the earl up the stairs and into the gaming rooms, where players in various stages of inebriation fondled painted women with shocking *décolletage*.

"What will it be, Tisdale?" asked Waverly. "Faro? Macao?"

"If it is all the same to you, sir, I have always wanted to try my luck at hazard," confessed his eager pupil.

"As you wish." The pair found a vacant table, the earl called for a pair of dice and a bottle of brandy, and the viscount's lessons commenced. The earl patiently explained the rules, then generously allowed his young protégé a few trial casts before play began in earnest.

The viscount won the first cast, a circumstance which he modestly ascribed to beginner's luck, but when the second and third also fell in his favor, he began to fancy himself a dab hand at the game.

"I trust you will give your professor an opportunity to win back his losses," remarked the earl, refilling the younger man's glass.

"Oh, of course!" the viscount consented generously, and play recommenced.

Alas, Lady Luck was in a flirtatious mood, and after losing four straight throws, he was obliged to break open his rouleau of guineas. The lead seesawed back and forth for some time thereafter, while the level of brandy remaining in the bottle dropped lower and lower, and the pile of guineas at the earl's elbow grew slowly but inexorably larger. It was not until a second bottle had been broached that the viscount looked down to discover that his rouleau of guineas had completely disappeared.

"I say, Waverly, thish ish — this is deuced awkward," he mumbled, pushing back his chair so that he might search underneath the table for his missing coins. "Can't think what might've happened to them."

"I believe they are all here, quite safe," Waverly said reassuringly, indicating the golden mound at his elbow. "Do not fret yourself over it, Tisdale. I must own myself a poor teacher indeed if your game does not begin to improve very soon. In the meantime, I shall be more than happy to accept your vowels."

The viscount blinked owlishly at the earl's winnings, and decided it would be insulting in the extreme to balk in the face of such generosity. He allowed the earl to refill his glass while he scrawled his initials onto an I.O.U. with an unsteady hand.

By the time they at last rose from the table, the second brandy bottle had been drained and the pile of vowels at the earl's elbow had reached an alarming height. When their sum was tallied and Tisdale found himself some five hundred pounds in debt, he was shocked into a state approaching sobriety.

"I — I don't have the blunt on hand at this moment," stammered the viscount. "Still, debt of honor and all that —"

"Nothing to worry about," Lord Waverly assured him, correctly interpreting his pigeon's blanched countenance. "You may have all the time you need to square things with your father."

Privately, the viscount suspected there was not that much time in a month of Sundays. Despite his own fondness for table and turf, the duke had no patience with his son and heir's indulging in similar vices. No, he could not go to the duke with a request for money, but there was another he could turn to — one to whom five hundred pounds would seem mere pocket change.

"I shall ashk — ask Nell," he said, more to himself than to the earl. "She musht — must be back soon. Can't see Nell staying in Manchester a minute longer than necessary. Depend upon it, that's the ticket."

The viscount had to wait four days for his sister's return. Being young and resilient, his body had by that time recovered from his excesses, but his mind was not so easily assuaged. What if his wealthy brother-in-law — no great lover of gaming, as he recalled — refused to cough up the ready? What if he were forced to turn to the cent-per-centers or, worse yet, his father? *When*, for God's sake, was Nell coming home? He only hoped that a prolonged sojourn with that Cit husband of hers hadn't put her in such a bad temper that she would refuse his request out of hand.

In this last, at least, the viscount's fears were unfounded. Far from returning to London out of temper, it was with an uncharacteristic sense of reluctance that Lady Helen returned at all. As the post-chaise bowled steadily southeastward, she found herself missing the easy camaraderie they had achieved in Lancashire. She darted a quick glance at her husband, who stared silently out his window at the landscape whizzing by, and wondered if he were thinking similar thoughts.

As if feeling her eyes upon him, he turned and gave his bride a tentative smile. "I'm afraid it wasn't much, as wedding trips go," he offered apologetically.

"I enjoyed it very much."

"You know, 'elen, I've been thinking," he continued hesitantly. "If you like, we could go somewhere after the Season ends — a belated wedding trip, per'aps. Not changing the terms of our agreement, or anything like that," he added quickly.

"That sounds lovely, Mr. Brundy." She started to suggest Italy or even Paris, now that the war was over, then remembered that, in either case, he could not speak the language. Not for the world would she embarrass him or make him feel ill at ease. "Brighton is always a popular choice for summer," she said at last.

"Then Brighton it is," he declared. "I'll 'ave me man of business locate a suitable 'ouse."

Their wedding trip settled to the satisfaction of both, they each returned to their own private thoughts. To be sure, Lady Helen had much to think about. She had once told her father that she did not know what she sought in a man, but was certain Mr. Brundy was not it. She could not have been more wrong. He was the man she had despaired of ever finding, and yet she had failed to recognize his worth.

But all of that was in the past. She knew now what a treasure was hers, and although he had not said it in so many words — and to be sure, she had given him no reason to feel thus — it seemed at times as if Mr. Brundy were rather fond of her. Perhaps, given time and opportunity, that fondness might grow into something deeper, something she dared not name, even to herself.

Accordingly, upon returning to the Grosvenor Square townhouse, she penned a note to her father's cook offering her husband's belated compliments on the salmon and requesting the receipt. While one footman delivered this epistle, another was instructed to remove all the extra leaves from the dining room table.

She had been home less than an hour when the viscount called, begging the indulgence of a private word with his sister. Correctly interpreting this request as a wish to speak to her without her husband present, Lady Helen instructed Evers to show the viscount to the drawing room, secure in the knowledge that Mr. Brundy would not emerge from his study before dinner.

"Nell!" cried young Tisdale, greeting his sister with outstretched arms. "I say, you're looking splendidly!"

He would have said that anyway, of course, to get into her good graces, but he discovered with surprise that it was true. She looked different, somehow, and although he could not have said precisely what the difference was, there seemed to be a certain glow about her that had been lacking before. Far from rendering her peevish, Manchester had obviously agreed with her.

"Teddy!" Lady Helen returned her sibling's embrace. "How are you? And how is Papa?"

"Oh, fine, fine!" the viscount assured her. "Papa is fine, too." *And I'm counting on you to see that he stays that way,* he might have added, but wisely refrained.

"You must tell me all the latest *on dits*. What has been happening while I was away?"

"Well, Miss Putney is to marry Lord Haversham, and rumor has it that Sir John

Haskell was forced to flee to the Continent to escape his creditors. And," he added, trying to sound nonchalant, "a new gaming house has opened in Jermyn Street. Went there myself one night to play hazard."

Lady Helen regarded her sibling with a knowing look. "Did you indeed? I'll wager it would be news to Papa!"

Thus discovered, the viscount abandoned all pretense of nonchalance. "Indeed, it would, and I am counting on you to keep the news from reaching his ears. I dipped a bit deep, and I'd drunk too much brandy, and — oh, say you'll help me! Please, Nell, I'm desperate!"

Lady Helen could not but be moved by her brother's despair. They had grown up concealing one another's worst peccadillos, when possible, from their father's wrath. "Who holds your vowels, Teddy? Can you not ask him to wait until quarter-day, or pay in installments?"

"I'd rather not, since Waverly was good enough to bring me along as his guest. I hate to impose further on his generosity —"

Lady Helen caught her breath. "Waverly? Are you saying *Lord Waverly* introduced you to this gaming house?"

"Yes, but —"

"He was not acting out of purely philanthropic motives, you may depend upon it. Any extra time he might allow you would come with strings attached. No, Lord Waverly must be paid at once. How much do you need?"

"Five hundred pounds."

"Five hundred pounds?" echoed his sister, aghast. "You call five hundred pounds a *bit deep?*"

"Come on, Nell," begged her brother. "I'll wager your pin money alone would support a small principality for a year!"

"I'll not deny that Mr. Brundy is more than generous, but five hundred pounds is hardly pin money!"

"No, but you could ask him for it, could you not?" coaxed her brother.

Lady Helen's glow flickered and died. "Pray don't ask such a thing of me, Teddy."

He had been braced for a show of temper, or even a diatribe on the dangers of frequenting gaming hells, but none of their childhood follies had prepared him for his sister's quiet misery.

"You don't think he would give you such a sum?" he asked.

"I don't know. I daresay he might, if I asked, but — but I don't want to ask."

By this time the viscount was growing seriously alarmed, for his sister's sake as well as his own. "Why not, Nell? Is he cruel to you?"

Lady Helen shook her head. "He is the kindest and best of men," she declared mournfully, in precisely the same tone she might have used had she professed him to be a monster of cruelty.

Still, her brother's countenance brightened. "There you are! If Brundy will cough up the ready, what's the problem? I vow, you're not yourself at all today." His eyes opened wide as one possible explanation for his sister's queer start occurred to him. "I say, Nell, you aren't in the family way, are you?"

"No," she said miserably.

"Then what's the matter?"

Lady Helen swallowed past the lump in her throat. "Mr. Brundy would think I only want him for his money."

Tisdale felt positively giddy with relief. "Is that all? You need have no fears upon that head, Nell. Mr. Brundy cut his wisdom teeth years ago. It's not like he thought he was making a love match."

Lady Helen's face flamed, and the viscount, observing his sister's heightened color, was moved to exclaim, "Oh, I say! Sits the wind in that quarter, does it?"

She made no reply, but nodded her head in the affirmative.

"Are you sure? I mean, he hardly seems your type, Nell. I always thought your tastes ran more to Lord Waverly and his ilk."

"He — does not show to advantage in London," admitted Lady Helen, feeling shamefully disloyal for doing so. "It was not until I saw him at his mill, among his own people, that I — that I came to — to care for him."

The viscount nodded in understanding. "Well, I must say, after the initial shock wore off, I thought he was a regular right 'un — for a Cit, that is."

"Teddy," replied his sister with great deliberation, "I will get your money for you, but only on two conditions: one, that you never go anywhere with Lord Waverly, and two, that you never, *ever*, refer to my husband in those terms again!"

Lord Tisdale accepted his sister's terms eagerly and, after professing (several times) his undying gratitude, took himself home to face his father with a much lighter heart. Lady Helen walked with him as far as the front door, then lingered alone in the hall long after he had gone, staring with unseeing eyes at the study door.

"And we were going to Brighton," she whispered sadly.

Dinner was not the pleasant occasion to which Lady Helen had looked forward with such eagerness. To be sure, her husband had smiled approvingly at her when he discovered that the dining room table had mysteriously shrunk, allowing them to dine in something approaching the intimacy they had enjoyed at Mr. Brundy's Lancashire residence. But Lady Helen could think only of the task which lay before her, and made only monosyllabic replies to his attempts at conversation, all the while plotting how best to wheedle him out of five hundred pounds.

"A penny for your thoughts," Mr. Brundy said at last, after yet another failed attempt to engage his wife in conversation.

Make it five hundred pounds, and I shall accept, thought Lady Helen. She shook her head. "You would find them overpriced, I fear. Since I am such poor company, I shall leave you to enjoy your port."

She would have suited the word to the deed, but Mr. Brundy rose with her. "I would prefer your company, 'elen, poor or no. Would you care to play piquet?"

To Lady Helen, who would ever after equate the card game with kisses, the invitation was almost too much to bear. "If you have no objection, Mr. Brundy, I think I should prefer to seek my bed."

"It's been a long day," he agreed, walking with her as far as the stairs. "I may be up very shortly meself. Good night, me dear."

"Good night, Mr. Brundy," she said, and made her solitary way up the stairs.

Barefooted and clad only in her nightrail, she followed a dark, cavelike tunnel, the candle in her hand providing the only light. As her eyes grew accustomed to the dimly lit cavern, she could make out nail-studded doors set at intervals along the tunnel walls, each one inlaid with a small barred window. As she passed one such door, a claw-like hand shot through the window and snatched at her hair. Suppressing the scream that rose in her throat, she hurried down the passage, unmindful of the wails and moans of the unfortunate souls imprisoned in the darkness. At last she reached her destination, where a cell door swung open before her as if by magic. Inside, Viscount Tisdale lay in chains, his hair and clothing filthy and his coltish frame gaunt and emaciated.

"Teddy!" she cried. "Teddy, what have they done to you?"

"Debt of honor," rasped the viscount, too weak to stand. "Couldn't pay. Waverly —"

"Lord Waverly did this to you?"

Her brother's answer was drowned out by the clang of metal on metal, and she whirled around to find that the cell door had slammed shut, imprisoning her with the viscount. As she gathered her breath to cry for help, a familiar, mocking face appeared in the tiny barred window.

"Welcome, Mrs. Brundy," drawled Lord Waverly.

Lady Helen screamed.

His wife's scream awakened Mr. Brundy from a sound sleep. Without lingering to don his dressing gown, he was out of bed like a shot, calling her name and pounding ineffectually at the connecting door. Receiving no response, he put his shoulder to the door and threw his weight against it. The door separated from its hinges with a creak of splintering wood. Mr. Brundy stepped over the debris littering the floor, flung back Lady Helen's bed curtains, and pulled her into his arms. Sitting on the edge of her bed, he rocked her gently, murmuring all the endearments he could not voice by day.

"'ush, love, it's all right," he crooned. "'Tis your own Ethan 'oo's got you now."

Still trembling, Lady Helen burrowed deeper into his embrace, and Mr. Brundy tried valiantly not to notice the lavender scent of her hair teasing his nostrils or the soft curves of her body pressed against his. Alas, he was but human, and not only did he notice all these things, he was compelled to act upon his knowledge. His lips brushed her hair in a light kiss, which led not unnaturally to another, and then another, and when Lady Helen raised her face to his, he was a lost man. His mouth claimed hers and she wrapped her arms around him and buried her fingers in his hair. With a groan, he pressed her back against the pillows and continued his gentle exploration of her mouth, her eyes, her throat. . . .

"Please, Mr. Brundy, st —"

At the sound of his wife's voice, Mr. Brundy's sanity reasserted itself. He released her on the instant, and sat bolt upright on the edge of the bed. "I — I beg your pardon," he stammered, his breath coming in labored gasps. "I 'ope you'll 'ave a peaceful night's rest from 'ere on out." *One of us might as well, for I won't shut me eyes again until morning,* he added mentally.

"Yes, I'm sure I shall," Lady Helen answered breathlessly. "Good night, Mr. Brundy."

Mr. Brundy would have returned to his own room, but as he reached the gaping hole left by his forced entry, his bare foot landed on a jagged sliver of wood. His curiosity piqued, he groped for the candle on Lady Helen's bedside table and fumbled with the flint. A moment later the candle flared to life, revealing the connecting door hanging drunkenly from its lower hinge. Scattered on the floor beneath it were the splintered remains of a delicate Sheraton chair. Mr. Brundy stooped to pick up a broken chair leg, then turned to address his wife.

"I may not be a gentleman, 'elen, but I'm a man of me word. I promised you six months, and six months you shall 'ave."

Without waiting for a reply, he blew out the candle and returned to his own room.

Alone in the darkness, Lady Helen lay flat on her back, staring up at the canopy overhead and thinking about what had just transpired. *Please, Mr. Brundy, stay with me.* The words had almost slipped out in spite of her best efforts to hold them back. What would he have thought if she had begged him to stay, only to demand a large sum of money the very next day? Why, that she had sold herself to him, of course, and not seen fit to inform him of the terms of the sale until after the transaction was complete! Sunk in despair, she rolled over and plumped up the pillows, then pulled the counterpane up over her ears. But when she closed her eyes, it was her husband's shoulder upon which her head rested, her husband's arms enfolding her as she slept.

Mr. Brundy, having reached the privacy of his own room, made his way to the washstand on wobbly legs. The urge to claim his conjugal rights was a physical ache, but only a blackguard would take advantage of a lady's distress in order to have his way with her — even if the lady in question were his wife. Not for the first time, he mentally calculated the time remaining. It was, he reflected, going to be a long four months, three weeks, and six days.

He had thought that sharing a platonic bed with his bride in a Warwickshire posting house was the worst torment he could endure. He had been wrong. Holding his wife, kissing her and feeling her slender body beneath him, had been a torture infinitely worse — and he wanted nothing more than to march back into her bedchamber and be tortured anew.

He picked up the pitcher from the washstand and filled the bowl with water. It had been steaming hot when it was first brought up, but that had been before dinner, and the water had long since cooled. Bracing himself against the cold, he plunged his head in.

11

If to her share some female errors fall,
Look on her face, and you'll forget 'em all.
ALEXANDER POPE, *The Rape of the Lock*

As dawn broke over Grosvenor Square, Sukey tiptoed into her mistress's bedchamber to clean the grate and light the fire. Upon seeing the condition of that usually immaculate salon, however, she almost dropped the ash can. The door which connected the mistress's bedchamber with that of the master had been broken down by force, and now hung crookedly from one hinge. The Sheraton chair, the placement of which had so shocked the little maid on the morning after the wedding, had been reduced to splinters, and the ruffled bed curtain had been partially ripped from its casing.

"Gor!" breathed Sukey and hastily retraced her steps back down to the kitchen, her task forgotten. "Mrs. Givens! Mrs. Givens! You'll never credit it, ma'am!"

Having assured herself of the housekeeper's undivided attention, Sukey proceeded to describe the scene upstairs in lurid detail, and was pleased to discover that, this time, her observations were not so easily dismissed.

"No!" cried Mrs. Givens, enthralled. "I'll not believe poor Mr. Brundy used his wife so shamefully, not for love nor money, I won't! And even if he did," she added in fine contradiction of her earlier protestations, "you may depend upon it that That Woman drove him to it! But of course he didn't, for he hasn't an unkind bone in his body, I'll be bound, and if you ask me, he's treated her far better than she deserves, be she the daughter of a duke or no! A full month married, and that chair still beneath the doorknob. It's not decent, I tell you!"

Mr. Brundy did not see his wife at breakfast, having an appointment with Messrs. Schweitzer and Davidson which took him to Cork Street before Lady Helen had yet arisen. In fact, most of the *ton* was still abed, and consequently he enjoyed (or rather, endured) the undivided attention of both the royal tailors. Having fended for himself for most of his life, Mr. Brundy found it difficult to submit passively as the two *artistes* dressed him in the new evening clothes which he would wear to Lady Randall's ball the following night. His patience, however, was at last rewarded when, after making the most minuscule of adjustments to his cravat, the two men stepped back and allowed him to view his reflection in the glass.

"Blimey!" uttered Mr. Brundy upon beholding the fashionably dressed stranger staring back at him. The black cutaway coat and pantaloons differed little in fabric or style from those he had worn on that fateful night at Covent Garden when he had first beheld Lady Helen Radney, but in the hands of the Regent's own tailors, the garments had been so cleverly cut as to appear molded to his form. While aesthetically pleasing, this was a cause of concern to the pragmatic Mr. Brundy.

"Will I be able to sit down?" he asked.

"Of course, of course!" Mr. Schweitzer assured him. "Jennings, a chair!"

Mr. Davidson surveyed his handiwork with a critical eye as his underling disappeared in search of a chair. "I do wish we might nip in the waist a bit," he said with a sigh of regret for what might have been. "Mr. Brundy, would you not consider a corset, lightly laced —"

"No!" said Mr. Brundy in that tone which wrought fear in the hearts of his workers, the more so because it was so rarely heard.

"There is nothing wrong with Mr. Brundy's waist," asserted Mr. Schweitzer, "although if I may say so, sir, a haircut would not be amiss."

"I daresay you're right," conceded Mr. Brundy. "I've not 'ad me 'air cut since I first left Lancashire."

"You will want a London barber, of course. Perhaps your valet might suggest a man."

"I 'aven't a valet, either."

"No valet?" echoed the tailor in shocked accents. "How, sir, do you propose to get that coat on unassisted?"

"I've dressed meself for twenty-eight years," Mr. Brundy pointed out reasonably. "'Tis unlikely I'll forget 'ow at this late date."

"But up to now, your coats have been of a decidedly inferior cut," objected Mr. Schweitzer. "Depend upon it, sir, you must have a valet."

Jennings, returning at that moment with a chair, froze momentarily as a thought struck him. In his line of work, he had seen many fashionable gentlemen come and go, and of one thing he was certain. The valet who could turn Mr. Brundy out as a beau of the first stare would be more than a success in his field; he would be a legend in his own time. As Mr. Brundy eased himself onto the chair, relieved to detect no signs of straining seams, the hireling picked up his discarded coat and, under the pretense of hanging and brushing it, appropriated the watch contained in the inside breast pocket.

Satisfied with his purchases, Mr. Brundy changed back into his morning coat and breeches, not noticing that his coat was somewhat the lighter. He inquired of Messrs. Schweitzer and Davidson when the remainder of his order might be completed, and upon being informed that it would be ready within the week, he took himself off. He had hardly reached the street, however, when he heard himself hailed in urgent accents.

"Mr. Brundy! Mr. Brundy, sir!"

Turning he saw Jennings, the tailors' underling, hurrying from the shop waving a shiny object in the air.

"Your watch, sir," panted the young man, dropping it into Mr. Brundy's outstretched hand.

"Thank you — Jennings, is it?"

"Yes, sir. Oh, and Mr. Brundy —"

"Yes?" he prompted when the hireling seemed reluctant to continue.

"I heard you might be in need of a valet, sir. I've never served a gentleman in his home, but I've dressed my share of them in the shop, and — and I'd turn you out in style without trying to turn you into a court-card. That is, I would if — if you'd give me a chance, sir."

Mr. Brundy studied his would-be valet for a long moment and then, satisfied with what he saw, nodded. "You shall 'ave that chance, Jennings." He withdrew a calling card from its case and scrawled his direction on the back. "After you square things with your employers, present yourself at Number 23 Grosvenor Square."

"Thank you, sir! Oh, and Mr. Brundy —" Again, a pause. "I don't want to work for you under false pretenses. You didn't leave your watch in there. I took it so I would have a reason to talk to you alone. I had every intention of returning it, whether you hired me or no," he added hastily.

Far from being offended, Mr. Brundy grinned at him. "Jennings, I've a feeling we're going to deal extremely well together — under one condition."

So great was his relief that Jennings would have agreed to any terms. "What's that, sir?"

"The day you try to stuff me into a corset is the day I turn you off without a character!"

From Cork Street Mr. Brundy made his way to Harley Street, where his dancing instructress awaited him in the music room. She was playing the pianoforte when the butler announced him, but broke off to greet him with a warm smile.

"Mr. Brundy! My favorite dancing partner!"

"Am I, now?" he asked, lightly clasping the hands she held out to him. "And 'ere I thought I could claim no better than second place in your esteem."

"Nor, for that matter, could I in yours," Lady Randall retorted playfully. "But I shall say no more on that head. Are you ready to begin? Very well."

As her ball was to be held the very next evening, Lady Randall had hoped to provide music for this their last session, but Mr. Brundy had been adamant in his desire for secrecy, and her suggestions that they hire a violinist or invite Miss Maplethorpe to play the pianoforte had met with steadfast resistance. Lady Randall had to content herself with marking time by counting aloud, and when it appeared that her pupil had mastered this skill, she suggested that he might find it beneficial to keep time in his head.

"After all," she said reasonably, "it would look distinctly odd if one were to whirl about the ballroom chanting '*one,* two, three, *one,* two, three,' again and again."

Mr. Brundy finding nothing to object to in this scheme, the next dance was conducted in silence. And so it was that, when Lord David Markham entered the music room unannounced, he was treated to the spectacle of his longtime inamorata in the arms of his best friend.

"Emily!" he cried, aghast. "And with Ethan, of all people! A man I would have trusted with my life!"

At the sound of his voice, the waltzing couple stepped quickly apart.

"I think I'd best be going," murmured Mr. Brundy, but Lord David moved to block the door.

"Are you a coward, then, as well as a philanderer?" demanded an outraged Lord David. "And to think I pitied you on your wedding day! I can see my pity was misplaced. It is your unfortunate wife who deserves my sympathy!"

"David, this is not what you think —" Lady Randall interposed, but only succeeded in drawing Lord David's wrath down upon herself. He reached her in two strides and seized her roughly by the shoulders.

"And you, madam! If you have conceived such a partiality for married men, why not marry *me?*

You may be sure I would honor my vows more than this blackguard has done!"

Lady Randall caught her breath, then asked very evenly, "Am I to take that as a formal offer of marriage, David?"

"Yes!" retorted Lord David, as if daring her to accept. "Yes, you are!"

"Very well," she said placidly. "I accept your generous, if somewhat obstreperous, offer."

Lord David merely blinked at her, the wind quite taken from his sails. "You do?"

"I do — as I would have done any time these past four years, had you but asked me."

Slowly, as one in a dream, he drew her into his arms. "Have I been a fool, Emily?"

"As a matter of fact, yes, but I shan't hold it against you," she said with a smile.

"I'm a younger son, and my prospects are no more than what I make them," he pointed out. "I felt I should establish myself in a career before asking you to share such a life."

"My dear misguided David, if Mr. Brundy did not let the workhouse stand in the way of his marrying a duke's daughter, I cannot for the life of me see why having an elder brother should prevent you from marrying a widow of independent means!"

"Then what I saw here — ?"

"What you saw here was a dancing lesson — one of many, actually. I would have told you, but Mr. Brundy particularly desired that it be kept secret, and I honored his wishes. He wants to waltz with his wife, David. In fact, he is so much in love with her that he could no more look at another woman than he could fly. You need have no fears on that head."

Lord David sighed. "I owe him an apology."

"I should say so."

"Devil take it, Ethan, I —"

He turned to address his wronged friend and benefactor, but save for himself and Lady Randall, the room was empty. Mr. Brundy, having the sense to know when his presence was no longer required or, in fact, even wished for, had long since made a discreet exit.

Upon returning to his domicile, Mr. Brundy headed straightway for his study. Here he calculated the wages of his new valet and dashed off a note to a barber of Jennings's recommendation, requesting that he call in Grosvenor Square the following afternoon for the purpose of giving Mr. Brundy a haircut. He was in the process of signing this missive when a light knock fell upon the study door.

"Come in," said Mr. Brundy without looking up.

The door opened, and Lady Helen advanced tentatively into the room.

"Mr. Brundy?"

At the sound of her voice, Mr. Brundy's attention was fully engaged. She looked, in his admittedly biased opinion, breathtakingly lovely in green sprigged muslin, but her demeanor was so self-conscious that Mr. Brundy's heart would have gone out to her, had he not lost it long since. He suspected she was thinking of that midnight encounter, and he wanted to set her at ease. He wanted to assure her that it had been none of her fault, and that she need not fear a repeat of the same. He wanted to bend her backwards over his desk and kiss her senseless. Instead, he settled for rising from his chair at her entrance.

"'elen! Come in."

"Are you very busy, Mr. Brundy?" she asked hesitantly. "I should not wish to interrupt —"

"No, no! You are always welcome, I assure you." Mr. Brundy hurried to close the door behind his wife, trying not to think of her in her nightdress with her honey-colored hair spilling about her shoulders. "'ow may I be of service to you?"

You may kiss me again, Lady Helen wanted to say. *And again, and again, and after that, there is a little matter of five hundred pounds. . . .* "I fear I have — quite unexpectedly — found myself in need of additional funds, and wonder if I might beg the indulgence of a — of an advance against next quarter's pin money."

"You need not *beg* me for anything," objected Mr. Brundy, seriously alarmed. "Is your allowance not sufficient? Should I increase — ?"

"No, no! Indeed, you are generous to a fault. 'Tis a — an isolated expenditure, never to be repeated, I assure you."

"Very well, if you're sure. 'ow much do you require?"

"Five hundred pounds."

Lady Helen braced herself for a thundering scold, or at the very least a lecture on the value of money, but none came. In fact, her husband, regarding her with raised eyebrows, looked more amused than angered.

"Five 'undred pounds?" he echoed. "All I 'ave is yours, 'elen, but before I surrender such a sum, is it too much to wonder where it is to be spent?"

"Of course not," she said with uncharacteristic meekness. She had expected the question, and had prepared for it accordingly, and yet she had hoped to the last that somehow she would be spared the necessity of telling a bald-faced lie. Unable to look him in the eye, she allowed her gaze to drop to the cluttered desktop — an unfortunate choice, as it landed on a carefully transcribed list of Brighton residences available for hire. Swallowing in order to moisten a mouth suddenly gone dry, Lady Helen continued. "I have recently learned of a — a charity school for orphans, and I was so impressed by the work done there that I somewhat rashly pledged a donation without consulting you."

"Far be it from me to stand in the way of your generosity, me dear," said Mr. Brundy. After retrieving a key from his desk drawer, he unlocked the wall safe and withdrew five crisp hundred-pound notes, which he presented to his wife. "There is one condition, 'owever."

That Mr. Brundy's cooperation might come with strings attached was a possibility that Lady Helen had not even considered. Whatever his terms, she was in no position to argue. "And what is that, Mr. Brundy?"

His smile was kindness itself. "You are to consider it a gift, not an advance."

"Thank you," Lady Helen said in a voice choked with emotion. "Thank you, *dear* Mr. Brundy!"

Seizing his rough weaver's hand in both her smooth aristocratic ones, she pressed it to her lips, then hurried from the room with her ill-gotten gain, leaving her bemused husband staring thoughtfully into space, nursing his hand to his cheek.

Upstairs in the privacy of her own room, she collapsed onto the bed and buried her face in her hands. She had lied to her husband, and that was bad enough, but to make matters worse, she had used trickery and deceit to turn one of the very qualities she most admired about him, that generosity of which she herself had so often been the recipient, against him. Like the veriest Delilah, she had arrayed herself in a particularly becoming gown which she knew to be his favorite color, and had come to him with a lie calculated to touch his heart and loosen his purse-strings — and she had not come away empty-handed.

Gradually, however, a new idea struck. It may have been a lie when she first told it, but it did not have to remain so. Leaping off the bed, she crossed the room to her dressing table and opened the little jeweled box where she kept her pin money. Quarter-day was still a month away, but Mr. Brundy was so open-handed that there was still a sizeable sum remaining. She tied it up in one of the monogrammed handkerchiefs she had received as a wedding gift, then after fetching a straw bonnet and pelisse from the clothespress, went downstairs to instruct the butler to have the carriage brought round.

Half an hour later, she was set down at a squat brick building in a squalid section of town. Resisting the urge to retreat to the security of the carriage, she marched gamely up the front steps and rapped sharply on a door marked "The Templeton Institute for the Education of Indigent Youths." A moment later the door was opened by a young girl whose threadbare apron and mended gown were nevertheless spotlessly clean and starched.

Lady Helen presented her card. "Lady Helen Brundy to see the headmaster," said the duke's daughter at her most regal

"Yes'm — right this way, my lady," stammered the round-eyed girl, overawed by the splendor of the unexpected visitor. She led the noble guest to a shabby office on the ground floor. "If ye'll have a seat, my lady, I'll fetch Mr. Templeton."

Lady Helen perched on the edge of a worn armchair and surveyed her surroundings. The light was insufficient for office work, but the desk was tidy and the bookshelves behind it well-organized, containing all manner of titles from scholarly treatises on education to Charles Perrault's *Tales of Mother Goose.*

"My lady?"

A worn-looking man of about sixty stood framed in the doorway, the weak sunlight from the windows reflecting off his spectacles. He was small of stature and his gray hair was thinning, but as he stepped closer Lady Helen could see that his pale blue eyes were gentle and mild. Yes, she had chosen the right place.

"How do you do," she said, offering her gloved hand.

"How may I be of service to you?" he asked. His handshake was firm, his manner respectful but not toadying.

"It is I who wish to be of service to you, Mr. Templeton," replied Lady Helen. "Since my marriage, I have become concerned about the welfare of poor children, particularly orphans. To this end, I have set myself a goal of donating five hundred pounds to your establishment."

Mr. Templeton's pale eyes bulged. "Five hundred pounds?"

"I regret that I cannot furnish you with the entire amount at present," she continued, fumbling in her reticule for the knotted handkerchief. "However, I hope this first installment will be of some use to you."

"In — indeed it will, my lady," stammered the schoolmaster, watching in awe as Lady Helen tugged at the knot to reveal the riches within.

"Words cannot adequately express my gratitude. Establishments such as this depend upon the liberality of people such as yourself to survive. Unfortunately, many of the aristocracy are so far removed from the sufferings of the poor that they feel no particular burden for them. If you will pardon my asking, what inspired you to give so generously?"

Lady Helen was silent for a long moment, and when she spoke, she did not look at him, but gazed pensively out the window. "My husband was not born to great wealth, Mr. Templeton. He came up through the workhouse, and now owns the cotton mill whose former owner was once paid to take him off the parish. If I am generous, it is because of the — the love — which I bear for him."

"I shall hope for the opportunity to meet your husband someday," said Mr. Templeton. "If I may say so, he sounds like a most remarkable man."

"He is," replied Lady Helen wistfully, smiling past the lump which had formed in her throat. "Very much so."

Lady Helen left the Templeton Institute with her purse considerably lighter; her heart, however, was less so. Although she was pleased that someone would benefit from her brother's foolishness (someone besides Lord Waverly, at any rate), she could not shake the feeling that even her voluntary penury was, at its heart, self-serving. For without funds to replace torn stockings, stained gloves, and the dancing slippers that would almost certainly be worn out the following night at Lady Randall's ball, she would be forced to virtually retire from Society until next quarter-day. And here, she discovered, was where her self-imposed penance fell short, for remaining cloistered at home would be no great sacrifice, so long as Mr. Brundy were there.

By the time she returned to Grosvenor Square, it was time to dress for dinner. Seeing no sign of her husband below, Lady Helen hurried up the stairs to her bedchamber to wash and change. As she entered the room, she reached for the bell pull to ring for hot water, but the sight which met her eyes drove such petty concerns from her mind.

The splintered wreckage of the ruined chair and the damaged door had been removed that morning, but while she had been visiting the Templeton Institute, the door had been replaced and a new lock installed.

On the table beside her bed lay a brass key.

12

Oh, what a tangled web we weave,
When first we practice to deceive!
SIR WALTER SCOTT, *Marmion*

Lady Helen stepped back to study her reflection in the glass. Since this ball was to be in honor of her recent nuptials, she had taken advantage of her married status to have a gown made up in a rich ruby-red shade that would have been considered fast, had she worn it a scant four weeks earlier. Although the lines of the dress were deceptively simple, the low-cut bodice was the tiniest bit daring, and the expanse of white bosom it revealed was ornamented with the magnificent diamond necklace which Mr. Brundy had given her on their wedding day. Her earrings were small diamond studs, so as not to fight with the necklace, and her hair was dressed high on her head, with tiny ringlets fringing her forehead and the nape of her neck.

Satisfied with her appearance, she dismissed her maid with a nod. As soon as the door closed behind the abigail, Lady Helen flew to the dressing table and removed the five hundred-pound notes from their jewelled hiding place. Pushing them securely to the bottom of her beaded reticule, she tugged the drawstring closed and looped the satin cords over her wrist, then sallied forth like a ship in full sail, prepared for whatever the night might bring.

At the top of the stairs, however, she drew up short. In the hall below, a man stood with his back to the staircase, his white-gloved hands clasped lightly behind his back. Although Lady Helen did not immediately recognize him, his well-cut formal attire bespoke the man of Quality. Her curiosity turned to outrage as the elegantly dressed stranger crossed the hall to the bowl of roses gracing a lacquered table beside the door and snapped off one of the dark red buds. Such presumption could not go unchallenged. Lady Helen judged it time to make her presence known.

"Look here, sir, what do you think you're — ?"

The unknown gentleman turned at the sound of her voice, and Lady Helen's gloved hand flew to her throat. At the foot of the stairs stood her own husband, smiling up at her as he tucked the rosebud into his buttonhole. Small wonder that she had not known him! Gone were the baggy, poorly cut evening clothes he had worn at Covent Garden; in their place were form-fitting black pantaloons and a coat that hugged his torso like a second skin. Beneath this sartorial masterpiece extended a watered silk waistcoat in a shade reminiscent of the finest French champagne. Gone, too, were the unruly curls, for his dark hair had been cropped in a fashionable Titus cut which needed no assistance from curling tongs.

Staring down at him, Lady Helen felt strangely bereft, as if the weaver she loved had suddenly been transformed into one of the Town beaux whose addresses she had once spurned.

"Mr. Brundy!" she cried, making her way unsteadily down the stairs on legs which suddenly balked at supporting her weight. "What have you done to yourself?"

"Only 'ad me 'air cut, and let the Dook introduce me to 'is tailors," he said modestly.

"But you look like — like —"

"Like a gentleman?"

The question, and the hopeful expression which accompanied it, were all the reassurance she needed. She should have known it would take more than a haircut and fine clothes to change her Mr. Brundy. She smiled down at him. "To the manner born."

He stepped forward to meet her, and the ostentatious diamond in his cravat flashed in the reflected light of the chandelier overhead.

"Still, there is one thing —"

"What is it, 'elen?"

"Mr. Brundy, would you mind removing your cravat pin?"

Mr. Brundy obliged, and Lady Helen likewise withdrew the tiny diamond stud from her left earlobe and inserted it through the starched folds of his cravat. There was something unexpectedly intimate about the act, and Lady Helen drew back, blushing.

"There," she pronounced, removing the remaining earring and dropping it into her reticule. "That's much better."

"Is it? I was told the stone was of the first water," Mr. Brundy said apologetically, for all the world like a chastened schoolboy.

"I'm sure it is," agreed Lady Helen quickly, unwilling to distress him. "It's just a bit — overpowering. You might consider having it reset, you know. I've no doubt it would be striking in a ring."

This suggestion found immediate favor. "I'll see Rundell and Bridge first thing tomorrow. Would you prefer a silver setting, or a gold?"

"I meant a *gentleman's* ring!" protested Lady Helen, alarmed that he had so misconstrued her meaning.

Mr. Brundy shook his head. "You've prettier 'ands, me dear."

The remark reminded Lady Helen of her wedding night, when she had shuddered at the touch of his work-roughened hands. Now, she reflected, she would willingly place her life in them.

"You'll spoil me, Mr. Brundy," she chided.

"I'm certainly going to try," promised her husband, and there was a warmth in his brown eyes which made her wish they might brave Lady Randall's wrath and stay home. They could play piquet as they had in Lancashire, and perhaps, if she were lucky, she might lose. . . .

This train of thought was interrupted by Evers, who came to inform Mr. Brundy that the carriage awaited his pleasure. Mr. Brundy draped her velvet cloak over her shoulders — a task which should have fallen to a servant, but one which he had appropriated for himself — and offered his arm to his wife. Lady Helen placed her gloved fingertips in the crook of his elbow, and together they descended the steps to the waiting vehicle.

As the guests of honor, the Brundys had been invited, along with some thirty other couples, to what Lady Randall termed an intimate dinner party preceding the ball. Consequently, Lady Helen saw her husband but little during dinner, for she was escorted to the table by Lord David Markham, who was acting as host, and was seated on his right. Mr. Brundy, despite the dubious distinction of being by far the lowest ranking male present, was nevertheless the guest of honor, and it fell to him to escort his hostess to dinner and claim the place of honor at her right, on the opposite end of the table from his wife.

Still, Lady Helen found her traitorous gaze wandering far too frequently to his end of the table. These longing glances were not lost on Lady Randall, who began to suspect that Mr. Brundy already occupied a much higher place in his wife's affections than he realized.

Events at the ball which followed seemed to

confirm her suspicions. As Lord David solicited Lady Helen's hand for the first waltz, he was brushed aside by his friend, who had earlier in the evening dismissed his attempts at apology as being unnecessary almost to the point of insult.

"You'll 'ave to wait your turn, David," said Mr. Brundy, taking his wife's arm. "'usband's privilege, you know."

Lady Helen made no protest, but allowed her husband to lead her onto the floor. In truth, she was too surprised to have uttered a protest even had one occurred to her. She had not forgotten Mr. Brundy's abrupt disappearance at Miss Pickering's ball, and until he claimed her hand, had not realized how much she had dreaded a repeat performance tonight. She remembered, too, how annoyed she had been on that earlier occasion at his lack of attentiveness. Good heavens! Had she loved him even then, and been too proud to admit it?

As they took their places on the floor, Lady Helen felt suddenly shy. She had waltzed countless times before with numerous partners, and although she knew that some still looked askance upon the new German dance which had taken London by storm, she had never quite seen what all the fuss was about. Now she knew. With Mr. Brundy's gloved left hand clasping hers, and the warm pressure of his right hand about her waist, it required only a very little imagination to be back in her bed in Grosvenor Square, locked in her husband's embrace with his lips on hers. . . .

Although the Brundys might have fancied themselves to be alone in the ballroom, they had an interested observer in the person of Lady Randall, who watched with a satisfied smile as her erstwhile pupil acquitted himself with surprising skill for one so recently introduced to the terpsichorean arts. She tried to catch his eye to communicate her approval of his performance, but soon gave up the attempt. Mr. Brundy, it seemed, had eyes for no one but the woman in his arms. The potential blow to Lady Randall's vanity, however, was warded off by Lord David, who came to claim her hand.

"Shall we join them?" he asked his intended bride, offering his arm.

Lady Emily shook her head. "The next dance, perhaps. Right now I am watching my pupil."

Accepting the snub without rancor, Lord David joined her in this activity, as did Sir Aubrey Tabor a moment later, still shaking his head in disbelief at the near loss of his one thousand pounds.

"That must be the *ton*'s most mismatched couple," he said, raising his quizzing glass to view the weaver and his aristocratic bride through a hideously magnified eye.

"Do you find them so?" asked Lady Randall. "I confess, I was just thinking how well they look together."

"They do, at that," seconded Lord David.

"And high time!" Sir Aubrey said. "I was beginning to debate the advisability of knocking

Ethan unconscious and dragging him bodily to my tailor."

"I believe Emily was referring not to the bridegroom's apparel, but to the mutual glow of connubial bliss," observed Lord David.

"Connubial bliss? Lady Helen?" scoffed Sir Aubrey. "Surely you jest! This was a marriage not merely of convenience, but of desperation."

Lady Randall regarded both gentlemen with a smug smile. "On the contrary, it was a love match from the first. The bride has just been a little slow to discover it."

Slow or not, Lady Helen was by this time fully aware of her feelings, and it was with regret that she heard the music end and stepped reluctantly out of Mr. Brundy's embrace. Still, it would be shockingly bad *ton* to dance every dance with one's husband, even if — or perhaps *especially* if — one had quite unexpectedly fallen deeply in love with him. She allowed him to escort her from the floor, where her brother waited to claim her for the next set. The sheen of perspiration coating the viscount's forehead testified to his nervous state.

"Waverly is here," he said as soon as they were out of Mr. Brundy's earshot. "Did you get the money?"

"I said I would, did I not?" Lady Helen answered testily, darting a quick glance over her shoulder to be certain her husband had not heard. " 'Tis in my reticule."

Viscount Tisdale blew out a relieved breath.

"When can you give it to me?"

"I shan't give it to you at all, Teddy. You might fritter it away in the card room."

The viscount was perhaps understandably offended. "I say, Nell, that's dashed unfair!"

"Unfair or no, I shall give Waverly the money myself." She thought of the scene in the study, and shuddered. "'Twas unpleasant enough asking Mr. Brundy for it the first time. I'll not risk having to do it again."

"You didn't tell him what it was for, did you, Nell?" asked her brother in some consternation. "If word gets back to Papa —"

"Have no fear, Teddy. Mr. Brundy believes I made a charitable donation to a school for orphans."

The viscount brightened visibly. "No wonder he gave it to you so easily! I must say, Nell, that was deuced clever of you!"

"It was utterly contemptible of me! But what's done is done, and it remains only to pay Waverly off. When we finish here, you may instruct him to ask me to dance."

This the viscount did, and a short time later, Lady Helen's hand was solicited by the earl. If Mr. Brundy's hackles rose at the sight of his wife being borne away on Lord Waverly's arm, there was nothing he could do to prevent it, as he was already promised to Lady Randall for the next set, and so Lady Helen was able to arrange her tryst uninterrupted.

"If you've no objection, my lord, may we sit

this one out?" she begged when Lord Waverly would have led her into the set. "I have something of — of a private nature to divulge which you may find of interest."

Lord Waverly bared his teeth in a wolfish grin. "But of course, Mrs. Brundy. I am, as ever, yours to command."

Taking her arm, he ushered her through a set of French doors opening onto a small balcony. He closed the doors securely behind him, then turned expectantly to face her.

"Now, what is this intimate secret you wish to reveal?"

Lady Helen opened her reticule and withdrew the five hundred-pound notes. "I have the money my brother owes you. If you are indeed mine to command, as you have long professed, you will oblige me by never gaming with him again."

Lord Waverly was all humility. "My dear Lady Helen, I beg your pardon! I never dreamed our, er, night of revelry would put you to such inconvenience."

"Do not try to gammon me, Waverly," advised Lady Helen, unimpressed with the earl's show of remorse. "Where else, pray, would he have gotten such a sum? You know my father well enough to know that he could expect no help from that quarter."

"Indeed, it appears I was not thinking clearly," Waverly confessed. "I do hope Mr. Brundy didn't cut up too stiff?"

"Mr. Brundy need not concern you," replied

Lady Helen in arctic tones.

"Oh, but he does," protested the earl, taking her chin in his hand and tipping her face up to meet his. "So long as he is married to you, my dear, he concerns me very much."

Lady Helen's eyes narrowed to glittering green slits. "Unhand me, Waverly."

"I think not," said the earl, and pulled her roughly into his embrace. "Admit it, Helen, I am the one you want! Why else would you have arranged this little *tête-à-tête* when your brother could have delivered the money just as easily, and without arousing the suspicions of a jealous husband?"

"Good God! You must be mad!" she accused, struggling in vain to free herself.

"And how can I be otherwise, when I see the woman who might have been my countess wedded to a misbegotten workhouse brat?"

Before she could avert her face, his lips claimed hers in a brutal kiss. Lady Helen fought with every ounce of strength she possessed, but her efforts only seemed to enflame him the more. She was able to free one hand, however, and when her efforts to pummel him into releasing her had no effect, she seized a handful of his carefully styled hair and pulled with all her might.

She found herself freed on the instant, and ran back into the ballroom before Waverly could renew his advances. Losing herself in the crowd, she made her way to the ladies' powder room where she might repair the damage to her person and recover her poise before seeking the security of her husband's presence. Having reached this sanctum, she scrubbed furiously at her bruised lips with the back of her hand, filled with irrational anger that Mr. Brundy's kiss was no longer the last to reside there.

She tucked a loose hairpin more securely in place and straightened the bodice of her gown, and was just about to return to the ballroom when the door opened to admit Mrs. Pickering, muttering over a rip in her flounced hem.

They exchanged polite greetings, and then Mrs. Pickering exclaimed, "Why, Lady Helen, whatever has happened to your lovely necklace?"

Lady Helen's horrified gaze flew to her reflection in the looking glass. The expanse of white flesh over the décolletage of her gown was bare. The necklace was gone.

"It — the clasp broke," she improvised rapidly. "It will have to be repaired."

"'Twould be a great pity to possess such a splendid piece and be unable to wear it," the colonel's wife clucked sympathetically.

Lady Helen vouchsafed a polite but meaningless reply and then returned to the ballroom, all the while hastily revising her plans. First she retraced her steps to the now-deserted balcony, where her suspicions were confirmed. Lord Waverly was long gone, and there was no sign of the necklace. She went back inside, but instead of seeking out her husband, she charted a direct course for her brother and practically ordered him to partner her in the waltz just beginning.

"I'm in the suds, Teddy," she confided under cover of the music. "I've lost the necklace Mr. Brundy gave me as a wedding gift, and I'm certain Lord Waverly has it. You must help me get it back!"

The viscount had been casting admiring eyes over the person of young Miss Pickering, and was understandably annoyed at being intercepted on his way to ask her to dance. "Confound it, Nell, it's not like you to be so careless! Why can't you just ask Lord Waverly to give it back?"

"I seriously doubt he would admit to having it in his possession."

"Why should he not?"

"Because I was fighting off his advances when I lost it!" was Lady Helen's indignant reply. "Depend upon it, he has it and he will find a way to make trouble unless I get it back."

"So how do you plan to do that?"

Lady Helen drew a deep breath. "I have a plan."

When she informed her sibling of this plan, however, he missed a step and trod heavily upon the train of a dashing young matron in indigo sarcenet, who shot him a dagger glance.

"Dash it, Nell," objected the viscount, "it ain't at all the thing, sneaking into a man's house in the dead of night!"

"I can hardly sneak into his house in broad

daylight," retorted his sister.

"Mr. Brundy won't like it."

This, in fact, was the only part of the plan which troubled Lady Helen. Suddenly it seemed that lie was piling on lie, and deception on deception. "No, he would not like it," she agreed, "and that is why he must know nothing about it. Please, Teddy, I need you to help me! After all, I wouldn't be in this fix if it hadn't been for you and your five hundred pounds!"

"All right, all right! I'll go with you to Waverly's house, Nell, but you'll wait in the carriage while I go inside and get the necklace."

"You wouldn't recognize my necklace if you saw it!" scoffed Lady Helen.

"Well, how many of the things do you think he's got in there?" retorted the viscount, stung.

At last the dance ended, and young Tisdale surrendered his sister to her partner for the following set. As the night progressed, one partner gave way to another, each recognizable only in that they were not her husband, until at last she felt a firm but gentle pressure on her arm, and heard her name spoken in a voice which could only belong to one person.

"I believe the next dance is mine, 'elen."

She allowed him to lead her back onto the floor, but the waltz had scarcely begun before Mr. Brundy deduced that all was not well with his wife. She hardly spoke, for one thing, and although they had conversed little enough during their first dance, she had at least looked at him.

Now her gaze remained focused somewhere in the vicinity of the earring she had fastened into his cravat.

"Is aught the matter, me dear?" he asked her at length.

Startled, she looked up, and the hunted expression in her eyes only served to strengthen his suspicions.

"Why, no!" she protested a bit too quickly. "What could possibly be the matter?"

"I was 'oping you would tell me," he confessed with a smile.

For just a moment, Lady Helen was sorely tempted. Every instinct urged her to make a full confession to this man who had proven himself eminently capable of handling anything life might choose to throw at him. Still, her tongue was kept tightly reined by the fear of seeing the concern in his eyes turn to — what? Disgust? Contempt? She could not bear the thought.

"Why, nothing is wrong," she insisted. "'Tis only the heat, and the crowd."

"Per'aps it will be less crowded in Brighton," suggested Mr. Brundy.

"Perhaps," she replied, but her answering smile was forced. Brighton had never seemed so far away.

13

If your descent is from heroic sires,
Show in your life a remnant of their fires.
NICOLAS BOILEAU-DESPRÉAUX,
Satire 5

It was after two o'clock in the morning by the time the Brundys returned from the ball. Lady Helen held her breath as they crossed the silent hall to the stairs, for the recently completed portrait which Mr. Brundy had commissioned upon their marriage now hung in the drawing room, and was clearly visible through the open doorway. Mr. Brundy had not noticed the absence of the necklace — or had not commented on it, in any case — and she did not want the painting to recall it to his attention. When they drew even with the door and he wheeled abruptly to face her, Lady Helen knew a moment's panic.

"Are you 'ungry, 'elen?" His expression, she was relieved to discover, was more like that of a truant schoolboy than a betrayed husband. "We might sneak down to the kitchen and raid the larder for a bite to eat."

The cozy image of eating cold meat and cheese

before the dying embers of the kitchen fire was almost too tempting to resist, but Lady Helen dared not yield. Her brother would be calling for her shortly, and she must be ready. Feigning weariness, she raised one gloved hand to her mouth to hide a contrived yawn.

"I vow, I can scarcely hold my eyes open," she protested. "Perhaps another time."

He shrugged. "As you wish."

Side by side, they climbed the stairs in silence, then Lady Helen paused before her bedchamber door.

"Good night. Mr. Brundy."

"Good night, 'elen. Sleep well, me dear." He brushed her cheek lightly with his lips, and it required the greatest effort on Lady Helen's part not to fling her arms around his neck and sob the whole sordid story onto his broad shoulder.

Once inside her room, Lady Helen sent her weary maid to bed and listened to the sounds emitting from the adjoining room. They were not difficult to discern, for Jennings, her husband's new valet, was bursting with conversation, and several minutes elapsed before the sounds ceased, indicating that the valet had been dismissed and Mr. Brundy had sought his bed. She glanced wistfully at the key lying on the bedside table and wished she possessed the fortitude to insert it into the lock, then snuffed out the candles in her own room so that he might not see the light under the door. After allowing sufficient time for her husband to fall asleep, she crept back down the stairs to await her brother.

Her patience was soon rewarded, for it was not long before the viscount's curricle drew up before the house. Wrapping her dark cloak more tightly about her person, Lady Helen opened the door and slipped out to meet her brother.

They said little on the short drive to the earl's Park Street house. Lady Helen, for her part, was beginning to have doubts as to the wisdom of her plan. What had seemed simple enough in a brightly lit ballroom surrounded by hundreds of people was quite another matter when undertaken alone in the dark hours before dawn. What if all the doors and windows were locked? One could hardly summon the butler to gain admittance for the purpose of searching his master's house. What if Lord Waverly had not even come home at all, but had spent the rest of the evening at his club? All too soon they reached the earl's house, and the viscount drew his curricle to a halt before a wide, pilastered façade.

"Now remember, Teddy," admonished his sister as she clambered down from the vehicle, "if I don't return in a reasonable period of time, you are to come in after me!"

The viscount nodding his assent, Lady Helen gamely mounted the steps to the earl's front door and tried the knob. To her surprise, it turned easily in her hand. It was, she reflected, almost as if Lord Waverly expected her. The thought was not a reassuring one. Opening the door a crack, she turned back to her brother, shrugged expressively at the unexpected boon, and entered the dark house.

Now, she thought as she carefully picked her way past artfully arranged bric-a-brac, if I wished to hide a diamond necklace, where would I put it? The first door opened onto a formal drawing room which Lady Helen immediately dismissed as too public; the second revealed a music room which, she suspected, was little used, Lord Waverly not being musically inclined. She cautiously climbed the stairs to search the more private rooms on the first floor, but as she reached the landing, cold fingers brushed her arm, and she uttered a tiny shriek in spite of her best efforts to stifle it. A closer look revealed a marble statue in the Greek style. Lady Helen gave a shaky laugh before continuing to the upper floor.

She inched her way along the passage until she felt a door, and here her hopes rose. Even in the dark, the room was decidedly masculine, as evidenced by the faint scent of brandy and tobacco which lingered in the air. Her groping fingers soon located a large desk on which sat a lamp. This she lit, and found herself in a study hung with dark green silk and decorated with framed hunting prints. It was the desk, however, that claimed her full attention. She pulled open the first drawer and rifled quickly through it. Finding nothing of interest, she was about to start on the second when a slight sound behind her made her breath catch in her throat. She turned and beheld the earl framed in the open doorway, still immaculately dressed in his evening attire.

"Welcome, Mrs. Brundy," he drawled.

They were the same words he had uttered in her dream, and spoken in the same world-weary tone. If, by screaming, she could have awakened to find herself safe in her husband's arms, Lady Helen would have shrieked the rafters down. But this was no dream, and Mr. Brundy was asleep in his bed in Grosvenor Square. The very thought conjured up an image so poignant it made her knees weak with longing. Still, her voice was remarkably composed as she said, "Good evening, my lord. Tonight at Lady Randall's ball I lost something which I believe to be in your possession. I would like to have it back, if you please."

She was prepared for protestations of ignorance, but to her surprise, Lord Waverly reached into the breast pocket of his coat and withdrew the necklace at once. "I trust it is this bauble to which you refer?"

"Yes, thank you."

She reached out to claim the prize, but Waverly moved it out of reach. "A moment, please. As it happens, I have need of this piece myself. I confess, it was a welcome instance of serendipity. I was at a loss as to how to rectify my, er, embarrassments without a protracted visit to the Continent."

"You have my sympathy, Waverly, but there is one thing you seem to have overlooked. The necklace is mine."

"Correction, my dear: it *was* yours. But in the

203

immortal words of the playwright, possession is eleven points in the law. Since the necklace is now in my possession, it remains only for me to decide how best to use it."

"You would not dare to break it up!" protested Lady Helen.

"Nothing so grossly mercenary, my dear," the earl assured her as he turned up the lamp, then moved to light the wall sconces. "There! So much cozier this way, is it not? As it happens, I made a quite unexpected discovery tonight, the ramifications of which I have yet to explore."

"And what, pray, might that be?" asked Lady Helen impatiently.

"You did not seem to welcome my, er, attentions, my dear. I had to ask myself why, and the only logical conclusion I could reach — although to call it 'logical' might be to put too fine a point on it — is that you have fallen in love with your weaver."

Lady Helen made no reply, but the glint in her eyes and the sudden lift of her chin told the earl all he needed to know.

"Shockingly bad *ton,* falling in love with one's spouse, but aside from that, it really is too ludicrous for words. Lady Helen Radney, the Ice Princess, melted at last. And by whom? A workhouse bastard!"

Lord Waverly had not expected to meet with violence, least of all at the hand of the icy daughter of the duke of Reddington, and so Lady

Helen's slap all but separated his head from his neck.

"You will regret that, my dear," he swore, rubbing his abused cheek. "So long as I have this trinket in my possession, I have the power to make you regret it very much. I wonder what our weaver would think if I were to wear this bauble as a lover's token? I could always hang it from my watch chain like a fob. Rather gaudy, I fear, but surely no worse than your esteemed husband's taste in cravat pins."

Lady Helen shrugged. "I don't know that he would care," she said with quite creditable nonchalance. "Since you have guessed my feelings for my husband, I must confess that I have no idea whether or not they are reciprocated. It is very lowering to admit it, but for all I know, he may be completely indifferent to me."

"If he is indifferent to you, my dear, then his lack of breeding is the least of his deficiencies. But cast your mind back to Covent Garden, and set your mind at ease. If it escaped your notice that your Mr. Brundy spent the better part of the second act gazing at you through his quizzing glass, I can only say that it did not escape mine. No, I do not think our besotted bridegroom would accept with equanimity the discovery that his bride of barely one month has already taken a lover."

Lady Helen's eyes narrowed. "All right, Waverly. What do you want?"

The earl stroked his chin, apparently wrestling with indecision. "Do you know, I cannot for the life of me decide. Do I want your own fair person, or your husband's fat purse? Fortunately, I see no reason why I cannot have both."

"I think you had best explain yourself."

"You know that I have for some time coveted, shall we say, a more intimate acquaintance with you. I think now you will be more receptive to the idea — so receptive, in fact, that you would not be unwilling to reward me monetarily from time to time for making you the object of my affections. In return, I shall keep this bauble locked securely in my safe, where your Mr. Brundy need never be distressed by it."

"I am afraid you are fair and far off, my lord. I have already told my brother I will not bleed my husband dry for his sake, and you may be doubly sure I will not do so for yours."

"Ah, but if you wish to remain in your husband's good graces, you had best rethink your position. I am sure we could —" He broke off abruptly as a knock sounded on the door. "Now, who the devil might that be?"

He strode impatiently to the study door and flung it open to reveal the butler, his coat and trousers thrown on hastily over his nightshirt. If he was at all surprised to see his master entertaining a young and unescorted woman at an hour long past that accepted for receiving callers, he certainly gave no sign.

"Begging your pardon, my lord," the butler intoned, "but Viscount Tisdale is below, and insists upon seeing your lordship."

"Ah, the brave rescuer, I have no doubt," said the earl to Lady Helen before turning back to his servant. "Very well, you may show young Galahad to the drawing room. I shall wait upon him directly."

"Very good, sir." The butler departed, leaving Lord Waverly alone with Lady Helen.

"Duty calls," he remarked with a heavy sigh. "Much as I hate to leave you, my dear, perhaps it is for the best. Some quiet contemplation might make you more inclined to listen to reason."

"I'm coming with you," said Lady Helen resolutely, following the earl to the door.

Lord Waverly was in the corridor by this time, but he turned back to address his captive through the crack in the door. "I'm afraid that won't be possible, Mrs. Brundy. You see, I always keep my valuables under lock and key."

Lady Helen sprang for the door, but Waverly was too swift for her. He shut the door just as she reached it, and a moment later she heard the click of the key turning in the lock.

Imprisoned in the study, she paced back and forth in helpless frustration, all the while keeping her clenched fists pressed tightly to her mouth. No matter how desperate her situation, she was determined not to give Lord Waverly the satisfaction of hearing her pound on the door or scream for help.

She knew her brother was downstairs working to effect her release, but too late she realized the futility of pitting a mere boy against a man of

Lord Waverly's cunning. No, her instincts had been right: she should have confessed the whole to Mr. Brundy while she had the chance. It seemed that she was destined to lose his good opinion in any case.

These melancholy thoughts were interrupted by a scratching sound emitting from behind the green velvet draperies as someone struggled to gain admittance to the house through the upper-story window. Far from being afraid, Lady Helen actually welcomed the opportunity of working off her pent-up energy on a housebreaker. After an evening of listening to the earl's veiled threats, dealing with a common criminal should be a simple enough undertaking. She crossed swiftly to the fireplace and seized the poker, then positioned herself before the window, her weapon hoisted high over her head.

Theodore, Viscount Tisdale, had had a bad feeling about this undertaking from the start, and never more so than when he watched his sister disappear into the bowels of Lord Waverly's darkened town house. As he awaited her return, the minutes seemed to crawl by, until he had no very clear idea of how long she had been gone. He had begun to debate the wisdom of going in after her when one of the upper-story windows suddenly blazed to life.

"Confound it, Nell, wouldn't a candle have been sufficient?" muttered the viscount under his breath.

A moment later, a shadow passed before the window, a shadow too tall and broad-shouldered to belong to his sister. Lady Helen, it seemed, had been discovered. He knew that, according to his sister's plan, he was supposed to come in search of her, but he realized now that such a plan had been doomed from the start. He was no more Waverly's equal at thievery than he had been at hazard. No, there was one far more capable than he of rescuing Lady Helen from her predicament — the one to whom they should have turned in the first place. Abandoning all thoughts of entering the earl's house, young Tisdale whipped up his horses and set out at a gallop for Grosvenor Square.

Drawing up before his sister's house, the viscount sprang down from his carriage, took the front steps two at a time, and began to pound on the door as if the Furies were at his heels. A moment later, the door was opened by Jennings, who, flushed with success from his first night as a valet, was still awake.

"Where is Mr. Brundy?" demanded the viscount.

"At this hour? He's in his bed asleep," returned the stunned valet.

"Well, wake him! I must see him at once!"

Jennings hesitated. "He might have my job if I do," he faltered.

"He'll have your head if you don't!" the viscount informed him roundly. "Now, are you going to wake him, or shall I do it myself?"

"I'm going! I'm going!"

Leaving young Tisdale in the hall, the fledgling valet mounted the stairs with the air of one approaching the guillotine.

"Hurry, man!" commanded the viscount.

Jennings accordingly picked up his pace, and a moment later Mr. Brundy descended the stairs, breeches and a dressing gown thrown hastily over his nightshirt. His hair was tousled and his eyes heavy from sleep.

"'ullo, Tisdale, what's toward?" he asked his brother-in-law.

The viscount wasted little time on pleasantries. "I'm sorry to disturb you at this hour, but you must know. Lord Waverly has got Nell."

"You've been dreaming, Theodore. 'elen is sound asleep in 'er own room. Believe me, I know," he added cryptically.

"I tell you, she isn't! I drove her to Waverly's house myself!"

Mr. Brundy was awake on the instant, all trace of weariness vanished. "What maggot got into your 'ead, that you would — ? No, don't answer that. Come upstairs, and you can tell me while I get dressed."

"Will you be needing my help, sir?" volunteered Jennings.

"No, take yourself back to bed — and if anyone asks, you slept soundly all night long."

Upstairs, Lord Tisdale gave a full account — interrupted by frequent apologies — of the circumstances which had led to his sister's entering the earl's house, while Mr. Brundy exchanged his dressing gown for a coat and waistcoat, and knotted a cravat carelessly about his neck.

"So you lost five 'undred pounds at 'azard," he concluded at the end of the viscount's speech. "Tell me, Theodore, were you playing against orphans, by any chance?"

"Orphans?" echoed the viscount, all at sea.

Mr. Brundy shook his head. "Never mind. Just take me to Waverly's 'ouse and stall 'is lordship while I get 'elen."

"Yes, sir!" said the viscount, who recognized the voice of authority when he heard it. "How am I to do that?"

"Get 'im to play cards. Lose as much as you please with me blessing, only keep Waverly busy!"

A short time later, Mr. Brundy watched from the shadows as his brother-in-law was admitted to Lord Waverly's house before stepping back into the street to study the upstairs window, where a light still burned. He shrugged off his baggy coat and knotted the sleeves around his waist — an act which would have reduced Messrs. Schweitzer and Davidson to tears, had it been perpetrated on one of their own masterpieces — then nimbly scaled the pilastered column nearest the front door to a tiny rounded balcony which formed the roof of the portico. Having achieved this objective, he flattened himself against the wall and inched along the narrow ledge fronting the house until he reached the lighted window. He then tried the lower sash and, finding it unlocked, pushed it up and crawled inside into a tangle of green velvet curtains. He was in the act of straightening up when something struck his skull with the force of a hammer. Stars exploded in his head, and he sagged against the curtains. They parted as if on cue and, deprived of this minimal support, he landed heavily on the carpet.

"Dear God!" came a woman's agonized cry. "I've killed him!"

14

Patience, and shuffle the cards.
MIGUEL DE CERVANTES,
Don Quixote de la Mancha

Dimly, through the pain in his head, Mr. Brundy recognized Lady Helen's voice, and wondered with detached curiosity whose death might have driven her to such despair. Before his overtaxed brain could supply an answer to this question, however, he slipped into delirium. In this befuddled state, he labored under the pleasant delusion that his abused head was cradled against his wife's bosom, and that she stroked his hair with gentle fingers. If this was dementia, he decided, there was much to be said in its favor. Hesitantly, lest the illusion vanish, he opened one eye.

"'elen?" he uttered thickly.

Far from disappearing, the vision gave a little gasp, and the green eyes regarded him with something approaching tenderness. "Oh, Mr. Brundy! Are you all right?"

"Never better," he assured her, smiling groggily through the pain. Reluctantly disengaging himself from his wife's arms, he held one hand to his throbbing head where a lump was already beginning to form.

"I'm so sorry! I didn't know it was you — I didn't expect you."

"I 'adn't planned on dropping in."

With this simple observation, the evils of Lady Helen's situation were forcibly borne in upon her. She rose to her feet, hugging arms which seemed strangely empty now that her husband no longer reposed there. "Yes, you — you must wonder bow I came to be here —" she stammered, studying the Axminster carpet with great interest. "I can explain —"

Mr. Brundy held up a hand to forestall her. "Spare me any more explanations, I beg you! I've 'eard more than enough from your brother already."

"Oh," said Lady Helen in a small voice. "You must be shocked and — and disgusted."

"Indeed, I am!" he answered in tones of revulsion. "If your brother can't 'old 'is own against a bunch of orphans, 'e'd best leave off playing 'azard altogether!"

Recognizing her own lie, Lady Helen hung her head. "You know it all, then. Still, I'm glad you came for the necklace, for Lord Waverly refuses to give it to me."

"I'm afraid you're mistaken, me dear. I didn't come for the necklace."

Up came Lady Helen's head. "You didn't?"

"No, 'elen, I came for me wife."

His tone was gentle, not accusing, and Lady Helen, who despised displays of excessive sensibility, was obliged to turn away so that he might not see her trembling lower lip and rapidly filling eyes.

"I do not deserve kindness at your hand, Mr. Brundy. I have used you abominably."

"Now, what's all this?" he chided gently as his fingers closed over her white shoulders. "'Tis only me 'ead, and it's 'ard enough." Receiving no answer save a stifled sob, he cut to the heart of the matter. "'elen, why didn't you tell me you needed the five 'undred pounds for your brother's gambling debts?"

"I wanted to, truly I did," she confessed. "I hated lying to you, but I — I couldn't bring myself to tell you the truth."

"In fact, I couldn't be trusted not to bear tales to the Dook," concluded Mr. Brundy.

This assumption was so glaringly abroad that she turned to face him in surprise. "No! That wasn't the way of it at all!"

"You didn't think I would give you such a sum?"

"That wasn't it, either. I didn't want to ask you for it because I — I couldn't bear for you to think that I had married you only for your money."

As that fact had been abundantly plain from the day he had first received permission to address her, Mr. Brundy had to smile at her distress. "Is that all? 'elen, why should I believe such a thing, when I 'ad it on good authority that you wed me because you found me preferable — but only slightly! — to 'iring yourself out as a governess or a paid companion?"

"You may wish I had opted for the governess's post when you hear what a fix I am in," she confessed. "Lord Waverly has the necklace, and he plans to use it to blackmail me. He has some notion of using it to convince you that he and I are lovers."

"It would take a great deal more than a trinket to make me believe that — or to make me wish you'd become a governess," he assured her.

"Yes, but there is no saying what he might do now, for I only made matters worse by slapping him, and —"

"You slapped Lord Waverly?" Mr. Brundy's dark eyes glittered dangerously. "And what did he do to you, that you were brought to such a pass?"

Lady Helen swallowed hard. "He called you a ba — a ba —"

"A what?" asked Mr. Brundy, all at sea.

"No lady can speak the word, Mr. Brundy!" she protested, blushing crimson.

Enlightenment dawned, and Mr. Brundy's ire gave way to amusement. "You can 'ardly strike a man for speaking the truth, 'elen," he pointed out reasonably.

"Oh?" challenged Lady Helen, every inch the duke's daughter. "Can I not?"

"Remind me never to provoke you to wrath,

me dear," said Mr. Brundy, utterly enthralled by the discovery that his wife had been moved to violence over a supposed slight to his honor. "We'll deal with Waverly momentarily, but first we must rescue your brother before 'e loses 'is shirt — or mine," he added darkly. "'e's downstairs playing cards with the earl, you know."

"But we can't get out. Lord Waverly locked me in."

"Then we'll get out the same way I got in," replied Mr. Brundy, striding back to the window.

"I can hardly climb down in a ball gown!" protested Lady Helen as her husband disappeared behind the curtains.

"You'll 'ave to jump for it, me dear," his voice came floating back to her.

"*Jump?*"

"Never fear, I'll catch you."

Lady Helen wavered between the fear of injury and the need to be near her husband before the latter won, and she looked out the window. Mr. Brundy had reached the ground safely and now stood on the sidewalk directly below, holding out his arms to receive her. She took a deep breath, then sat down on the window sill, gathered up her skirts, and swung her legs out, unintentionally treating her appreciative husband to the sight of slender white-stockinged calves tied at the knee with satin garters.

"Here I come," she called, and pushed herself off.

As Lady Helen was rather tall, perhaps she

weighed more than Mr. Brundy had expected, or perhaps he was momentarily distracted by the enchanting view afforded him. At any rate, he did indeed catch Lady Helen, but the force of her descent all but knocked him to the pavement, and the jolt caused his injured head to throb anew.

Lady Helen, tugging at the skirts which had by this time bunched up over her knees, saw him wince. "Oh, dear! Your head must ache dreadfully."

"Not at all," he lied, setting her on her feet.

He untied his coat from about his waist and shrugged it back on, then drew his wife's hand through his arm and strode boldly up the stairs to knock at the earl's front door.

"Are you sure this is wise, Mr. Brundy?" asked Lady Helen.

"Chin up, me dear," he said, giving her hand a reassuring squeeze as they waited for the butler to answer. "We'll come about all right."

A moment later they were ushered into the drawing room by a curiously dressed butler who had by this time abandoned all expectation of slumber.

"Mr. Ethan Brundy and Lady Helen Brundy," he announced woodenly.

As Mr. Brundy had predicted, the earl and the viscount sat playing cards before a hastily lit fire. A half-filled brandy decanter occupied one corner of the card table and a glass sat at each player's elbow, although the viscount's appeared

218

to be untouched. The pile of guineas before the earl's place, Mr. Brundy noted wryly, testified that young Tisdale had taken his brother-in-law's blessing to heart.

At the announcement of the new arrivals, the viscount's face registered patent relief. Lord Waverly, however, was not so pleased. A singularly ugly expression ever so briefly darkened his handsome countenance before his face assumed a mask of icy politeness.

"Why, Mr. Brundy, I must confess I had never pictured you in the rôle of romantic hero," he drawled. "I must say you wear it surprisingly well — a pity the same cannot be said for that coat."

Mr. Brundy made no response to this statement, but addressed the earl just as if he were paying a morning call. "Good evening, your lordship, or should I say good morning? I 'ate to bother you at this hour, but me wife is convinced you 'ave in your possession a necklace which she lost tonight at Lady Randall's ball."

The earl's face registered incredulity. "Lady Helen *lost* her necklace? I realize how this must pain you, Mr. Brundy, but the lady presented it to me just this evening as a token of her, shall we say, affection."

"This is news, indeed!" said Mr. Brundy, turning to his wife in feigned surprise. "'ave you any affection for Lord Waverly, me dear?"

"None whatsoever," stated Lady Helen in no uncertain terms.

"There you are," Mr. Brundy addressed his host. "An unfortunate misunderstanding, per'aps, but no real 'arm done. If you'll return the necklace to me wife, we'll impose no longer on your 'ospitality."

Lord Waverly withdrew the necklace from his coat pocket and laid it before him on the card table. "I have a better idea," he said with great deliberation. "I say it was a gift; Lady Helen says it was not. Since it is a matter of my word against hers, we shall settle it in the only fair way. I shall play you for it, Mr. Brundy."

"Done," said Mr. Brundy without hesitation.

Lady Helen gave an audible gasp.

The earl idly shuffled the deck of cards on the table before him. "Have you a preference of game?"

"I've recently conceived a fondness for piquet," confessed Mr. Brundy, with a secret smile for his wife.

"Don't do it, Mr. Brundy," pleaded Lady Helen, who had not forgotten her husband's abysmal performance in Lancashire. "Let him keep the necklace and say what he will. 'Tis doubtful anyone will take him seriously, in any case."

"There I must disagree, me dear," said Mr. Brundy, with steel in his voice. "When someone tries first to blackmail and then to slander me wife, I take it very seriously indeed."

"In that case, you have only to name your stake, Mr. Brundy," Lord Waverly said. "But what will it be? To be brutally honest, I can't think of anything you have that I would want."

"I can think of one, but I've a fancy to keep 'er," said Mr. Brundy, glancing at his wife. "I've a cotton mill, though, just north of Manchester —"

"No!" cried Lady Helen, flinging her arms about his neck. "Not your mill, Mr. Brundy, you mustn't! I won't let you!"

"You *won't let me*, 'elen?" echoed Mr. Brundy, gently but firmly disengaging himself from his wife's embrace. "I should 'ate for us to 'ave our first quarrel right 'ere in front of 'is lordship."

"But — but if you should lose your mill —"

"I've not lost anything yet," pointed out Mr. Brundy, ever the voice of reason. "Theodore, take your sister 'ome and stay with 'er until I return."

The viscount, who had been listening to the exchange up to this point with wide eyes and a slackened jaw, sprang to life. "Yes, sir!"

But Lady Helen refused to be budged. "I won't leave you!" she declared, clinging to her husband's arm.

"And very nervous I would be, with you watching over me shoulder to make sure I played me cards right," he replied. "Lord Waverly, if you'll excuse me for a moment, I'll see me wife on 'er way 'ome."

Lord Waverly sketched an elaborate bow. "I await your convenience, Mr. Brundy."

"Come, me dear." Mr. Brundy put his arm

about his wife's shoulders and propelled her toward the door, leaving the viscount to bring up the rear. Outside, Tisdale climbed into his curricle and took the reins, and Mr. Brundy handed Lady Helen up beside him.

"Please, *please* don't play Lord Waverly," she implored, clutching at his sleeve.

"I must, 'elen."

"But what if —"

"Buck up, me dear. I'll be 'ome soon."

"I love you, Mr. Brundy," blurted out Lady Helen.

Mr. Brundy looked at her for a long moment, then picked up one of the cold hands gripping his sleeve and carried it to his lips.

"Then whether I win or lose, I'll still be the richest man in England," he said, and gave the viscount the signal to drive on.

He watched the departing curricle until darkness swallowed up the pale oval of his wife's face, then turned back toward the house and found Lord Waverly observing the proceedings from the portico.

"A vastly touching scene," drawled the earl. "I wonder if she will feel the same when you return to her destitute."

"I'm sure you would love to find out," remarked Mr. Brundy, following Waverly back into the house.

"Alas, I fear I already know the answer," said the earl with a sigh. "Lady Helen's standards have slipped sadly since her marriage. I cannot feel you to have been a good influence on her."

Mr. Brundy bowed his appreciation. "Coming from you, me lord, I'll take that as a compliment."

"It was not intended as such, believe me."

Mr. Brundy assumed the viscount's vacated seat, and the two men faced each other across the card table, the jaded debauchery of the old order against the brash vitality of the new.

"Drink up, Mr. Brundy," instructed the earl, pouring a glass of brandy for his guest. "It has been a long evening."

"Would it contain 'emlock, by any chance?"

"Alas, no. I had none, nor arsenic neither. Believe me, had I known I would have the pleasure of entertaining you, Mr. Brundy, I should have been better prepared."

Mr. Brundy had no fears of being poisoned, but he had no doubt the earl would not hesitate to try and drink him under the table. Tempting though it might be to let the potent liquid deaden the throbbing ache in his head, he had no intention of letting liquor cloud his judgement. His wife, between her poker and her parting words, had clouded it quite enough already.

"I understand 'elen was a bit overeager in me defense," remarked Mr. Brundy as the cards were cut and dealt. "I trust you'll not 'old it against 'er."

"Not at all," Lord Waverly assured him smoothly. "I admire a woman of spirit."

"Aye, so do I. But I'm afraid you'll 'ave to find your own, Waverly. 'elen is already married — to me."

"Married? Purchased, more like!" spat the earl.

"Forgive me, but I'm a bit slow tonight," said Mr. Brundy, kneading the lump on his head. "Do you despise me for me money, or me wife?"

One eyebrow arched toward Waverly's hairline. "My good fellow, had you not married Lady Helen Radney, I would never have deigned to notice you at all."

Mr. Brundy nodded in understanding. "'Tis me wife, then. I can 'ardly blame you. I've no doubt I should feel the same about you, 'ad she married you instead."

Each man having arranged his cards to his satisfaction, the first stage of play, the calling, began.

"Five," declared the earl, and awaited his opponent's response.

"Good," said Mr. Brundy with a sigh, and Waverly scored the points.

"Four," Waverly continued.

Mr. Brundy inspected the cards in his hand and replied, "Equal."

"Do you really think so, Mr. Brundy?" sneered the earl. "To be sure, some may argue that you have belied the old adage and made a silk purse out of a sow's ear, but alas, a sow's ear, in whatever form, is still a sow's ear."

Mr. Brundy felt compelled to object. "I'm

224

afraid you've made a mistake, me lord. I'm in cotton, not silk."

"Make no mistake about this, Mr. Brundy," said the earl with great deliberation, peering malevolently over his cards. "Nothing would give me greater pleasure than to toss you back into the gutter from whence you sprang."

"Then you'd best mind your play," recommended Mr. Brundy, scoring the point.

This the earl did, and took the next three tricks, scoring a point for each.

"I shan't know what to do with a cotton mill," he remarked at length. "It would never do for a Waverly to soil himself with Trade. Should I sell it, do you think, or shall I dismantle it brick by brick as an example to ambitious weavers who don't know their station?"

His opponent merely shrugged. "Provided you win, me lord, that decision will be entirely up to you. Still, if you care for 'elen at all, I wonder at your eagerness to reduce 'er to penury."

"Fear not, Mr. Brundy. Lady Helen will not go begging, I assure you."

Mr. Brundy, pinning the earl with a look, did not pretend to mistake his meaning. "Not while there's breath in me body."

And so it went, through six hands. Mr. Brundy's head pounded mercilessly, making concentration difficult. By the time the last trick was taken, he had long since lost any feel for who might be leading. Not until the points were totaled would he know whether or not the mill was still his.

"Do you wish to tally the points, me lord, or shall I?" he asked.

"By all means, go ahead," said the earl, bowing his acquiescence. "You will no doubt wish to see the task completed quickly so that you may hurry home to comfort your wife, and since you work with figures daily, you are no doubt more adept at the skill. A gentleman, as you may have heard, leaves such mundane tasks to his steward."

"Then I 'ope, for your sake, that your steward is a man you can trust," replied Mr. Brundy, and set to work with pen and paper. A few moments later he laid the pen aside and pushed the paper across the table for the earl's perusal.

As Lord Waverly surveyed the sums at the bottom of the sheet, his face grew dark with impotent fury. "I don't believe it!"

"Shall I 'ave the butler summon your steward?" offered Mr. Brundy.

Ignoring this suggestion, the earl picked up the pen and, despite his professed lack of practice, soon arrived at the same conclusion.

"Take it!" he snarled, hurling the diamond necklace across the table at his opponent. "And may you rot in hell with it!"

"I should not dream of intruding upon you there," replied Mr. Brundy, bowing deeply from the waist. Then he pocketed the diamonds and quitted the room.

Once outside, Mr. Brundy stepped into the gaslit street and took a deep breath. The pain in his head had disappeared as if by magic, and for the first time since the viscount had pounded on his door, he allowed himself to feel the full range of emotions which, in the interest of keeping a level head, he had held firmly in check all evening: the horror of knowing that the woman he loved was in danger, and the relief of finding her unharmed; the cold fury that had made him long to inflict bodily injury upon Lord Waverly, and the wonder of knowing that Lady Helen had already done so, and in his defense; the fear of losing the mill, and the satisfaction of discovering himself the winner by a scant four points. And most of all, the sheer, giddy elation of hearing his wife's parting words. She would no doubt be frantic with worry by now, but since she and her brother had taken the curricle, he was forced to prolong her agony while he walked home.

A crossing sweeper plied his trade on the corner in the hopes of being rewarded by those members of the nobility returning home in the wee hours after a night of merriment. Mr. Brundy, in charity with the whole world, did not disappoint him.

"'ave you a wife, me good man?" he asked the sweeper.

"Aye, guvnor, that I do," was the reply.

"You 'ave me 'eartiest congratulations," said Mr. Brundy, tossing the man a crown piece.

"Thankee, sir," the sweeper said, tugging on his forelock. "And a pleasant evening to you and your lady wife."

He hastily swept a path for his benefactor to cross, but he need not have bothered, for Mr. Brundy was hardly aware of the pavement beneath his feet. He was going home to his lady wife, who loved him.

15

Love . . . levels all ranks,
and lays the shepherd's crook
Beside the scepter.
EDWARD BULWER-LYTTON,
The Lady of Lyons

"What can be keeping him so long?" Lady Helen wondered aloud as she restlessly paced the drawing room, her skirts flaring about her in a swirl of ruby red satin each time she changed direction.

"They do have six hands to play, you know," pointed out her brother from his vantage point on the sofa.

"If he loses his mill, I shall never forgive myself," declared Lady Helen, not for the first time.

"Confound it, Nell, have a little faith in your husband," the viscount admonished his sister. "Seems to me we've underestimated the fellow. For all you know, he might win."

"We played piquet one night in Lancashire, Teddy," she confessed, neglecting to mention the stakes on that particular occasion. "I won."

The viscount let out a long, low whistle, an unflattering estimation of his sister's skill at cards. "Even if he does lose the mill, he'll hardly be destitute," he argued, struggling for something positive to say. "Papa had him investigated quite thoroughly before giving him permission to address you, and it seems he has a respectable income just from his dealings on 'Change."

Lady Helen shook her head. "It isn't just the money, Teddy. That mill means the world to him. I'll never forgive myself if he loses it because of me," she said yet again, making another circuit around the room.

"It isn't your fault, Nell," Tisdale said soothingly.

This was perhaps an unfortunate observation, as it reminded Lady Helen of the true author of her distress. "Quite right, Teddy. It's *your* fault, and I'll never forgive you, either."

Thus chastened, the viscount abandoned his rôle as comforter. But without the well-meaning interruptions of her brother, Lady Helen's imagination was free to wander where it would, and her thoughts immediately took a downward turn. If fortunes could be made on the Exchange, they could be lost there as well. Perhaps her husband was more dependent on the mill for his livelihood than her father's sources had realized. Perhaps, after a brief, cruel taste of prosperity, he was about to be thrown back upon the parish. Well, she determined, if he returned to the workhouse, he would not go alone. She was still his wife, for richer, for poorer, and she would follow him to the ends of the earth.

Her pacing came to an abrupt halt when she

heard the front door open and then close. Measured footsteps echoed across the hall, and a moment later Mr. Brundy appeared in the doorway. He looked weary to the point of exhaustion, but his brown eyes blazed with a light which could have been anything from the fevered glow of victory to the half-crazed despair of a ruined man. His hands, she noted with a growing sense of dread, were empty.

She would have rushed to comfort him, but her feet refused to go forward, and when she spoke, her voice was little more than a whisper.

"Mr. Brundy?"

Without a word, he advanced into the room and moved to stand behind her. Then, withdrawing the necklace from the breast pocket of his coat, he draped it around her neck and fastened the clasp. The last vestige of Lady Helen's self-possession fled. She buried her face in her hands and burst into great, wrenching sobs that shook her whole body.

"'ush, now, love, it's all over and no 'arm done," murmured Mr. Brundy, drawing her into his arms and holding her close.

"I say, dashed fine show!" exclaimed the viscount, leaping to his feet to congratulate his brother-in-law. "You must tell me how you did it!"

"Tomorrow, per'aps, but not now," replied Mr. Brundy in a voice that brooked no argument. "Much as I enjoy your company, Theodore, I think I've 'ad me fill of it for one night."

Tisdale's wide-eyed gaze shifted from Mr. Brundy to the weeping woman in his arms, and back again. "Right-o!" he said with a broad grin, taking his abrupt dismissal in the spirit in which it was intended. "Until tomorrow, then!"

Mr. Brundy continued to hold his wife long after the viscount had gone, murmuring endearments into her ear and drinking in the lavender scent of the honey-colored tendrils tickling his nose. At length, her tears ceased to flow, and she raised her eyes to his.

"Oh, Mr. Brundy, however did you manage it?" she asked.

He merely shrugged. "Just because I don't choose to gamble doesn't mean I don't know 'ow."

"But when we played piquet in Lancashire, you were *dreadful!*" insisted Lady Helen.

"'aven't you guessed, love? I let you win that night."

"Oh." As she digested the implications of this disclosure, Lady Helen stiffened in his embrace. "In fact, you didn't *want* to kiss me."

"Is that what you think, 'elen?"

The look in his eyes made her heart beat unaccountably faster, and she let her gaze drop to the top button of his waistcoat. "Truth to tell, I don't know quite *what* to think of you, Mr. Brundy. Papa said you desired an aristocratic wife to solidify your position in Society, but you have never appeared to me to be overly concerned with Society's opinion of you. To be sure, you have never been anything but good to me, but the same may be said of the way you treat your workers —"

"I've never treated any of my workers like this," objected Mr. Brundy, pulling her none too gently into his arms and kissing her in a way that left no doubts as to the violence of his affections.

"Oh!" said Lady Helen unsteadily, when she could speak at all. "Lord Waverly said that you were — were not indifferent to me."

"Not indifferent to you?" he echoed incredulously.

"I believe 'besotted' was the word he used," she confessed.

"For once, I find meself in complete agreement with 'is lordship. I've loved you from the moment I saw you, 'elen. I took one look at you and it was bellows to mend, and no mistake. Made a regular cake of meself, I did, vowing on the spot that I was going to marry you and browbeating poor David Markham into introducing me."

Lady Helen flinched at the memory of her own behavior on that occasion. "And I was perfectly beastly to you!"

"And why shouldn't you be? You were used to 'obnobbing with peers of the realm, not work'ouse brats. 'ad it not been for me, you would've married a dook or an earl with a title to match your own."

"I can think of no title I should covet so much as that of Mrs. Brundy," said Lady Helen.

"Still and all, love, I'll never be a fine gentleman like your other suitors."

"That's not true!" she protested, emphasizing the point by clinging rather closer. "You have always been a gentleman in the noblest and best sense of the word, and — and you are the finest person I've ever known, Mr. Brundy."

"Do you know, 'elen, it's become something of an ambition of mine to 'ear me given name on your lips?"

"And do you always achieve your ambitions, Mr. Brundy?" she asked breathlessly.

"Always, up to now. Please, 'elen. 'Tis the only name I can offer you that's truly me own."

"Very well — Ethan," whispered Lady Helen.

"Say it again," he commanded, and although his tone was playful, there was a light in his eyes which would not be denied.

"Ethan," she repeated, with more conviction.

"Louder."

"Ethan," she said a third time, laughing at the absurdity of it all.

Mr. Brundy, having at last heard his name upon her lips, lost no more time in kissing it off. Alas, this pleasant enterprise came to an abrupt end when Lady Helen pulled away.

"Oh, Mr. Brun — that is, Ethan, darling! — I've a confession to make."

"What is it, love?"

"About that five hundred pounds —"

"Pray don't think of it again," insisted her husband.

"Oh, but I must! You see, I felt so perfectly dreadful about lying to you that I donated all my pin money to a school for orphans, and so if I am to replace my dancing slippers or buy new gloves or — or anything of that nature, I am completely at your mercy."

Mr. Brundy took a moment to contemplate the strength of his position before asking, "Completely at me mercy, you say?"

Lady Helen nodded.

"And if I've none?"

"Then I suppose I must economize by remaining quietly at home until next quarter day."

"That settles it! You'll not 'ave a brass farthing out of me," declared Mr. Brundy, softening the blow, however, by kissing her again.

"Well, then," said Lady Helen with uncharacteristic shyness, "since it seems I am to have a great deal of time on my hands, perhaps —"

Finding her reluctant to continue, he prompted, "Per'aps what, love?"

She took a deep breath. "Perhaps we need not wait a *full* six months, after all."

Gripping her shoulders, he looked intently into her green eyes. "Are you sure?"

Her color was high, but her voice was steady. "Quite sure, Ethan."

Mr. Brundy needed no further invitation. Without a word, he swept his wife up in his arms and started for the stairs.

As dawn cast its gray light over Mayfair, Sukey

tiptoed into her mistress's bedchamber to clean the grate and light the fire. She was brought up short by the sight of Lady Helen's undisturbed bed and the fine linen nightdress spread out, untouched, on the counterpane. My lady, it seemed, had flown the nest.

Self-preservation struggled with duty as Sukey vacillated on what course of action to take. Should she risk a beating and waken the master to inform him of his wife's defection, or should she keep a still tongue in her head, and risk a beating when he discovered she had known all along? To be sure, Mrs. Givens might swear that he hadn't an unkind bone in his body, but then, *her* position was secure. In the end, however, duty carried the day, and Sukey picked up the key from Lady Helen's bedside table, unlocked the connecting door into the master's bed-chamber, and silently turned the knob.

Her jaw dropped at the sight which met her eyes. My lady's magnificent diamond necklace lay on the table beside the bed, along with a number of hairpins. The bed curtains were drawn tightly shut, but the sounds of soft sighs and deep, satiated breathing emitting from within betrayed the presence of more than one sleeping inhabitant. Most telling of all, the carpet was littered with Mr. Brundy's coat, waistcoat, breeches, shirt, and cravat — along with Lady Helen's ruby-red gown, petticoat, shift, white silk stockings, and dainty satin garters.

As the significance of her discovery began to

dawn, Sukey's ash can slid to the floor un-noticed, and she ran from the room.

"Mrs. Givens! Mrs. Givens!" she shrieked as she clattered down the back stairs. "You'll never credit it, ma'am, I'll *swear* you won't!"